TEXAS DAWN

TEXAS DAWN

•

Cheri Jetton

AVALON BOOKS
NEW YORK

PRINTED IN THE UNITED STATES OF AMERICA
ON ACID-FREE PAPER
BY HADDON CRAFTSMEN, BLOOMSBURG, PENNSYLVANIA

This one is for Caprice, my firstborn,
who loaned me one of her previous jobs and grumpy bosses.
It's also for *Vancy-pants* and the littlest of angels.

Acknowledgments

I'd like to thank Francyne Anderson, one of my first mentors in RWA, for insisting I tone down my grumpy hero—again, and again, and again! Thanks also to Pam Mellor, my critique partner, who poked and prodded me through many a manuscript, as well as to author Jan Hudson who shared with me *the secret* of publishing success—PERSEVERANCE. Thank you all for your generosity.

Chapter One

No turning back now. Dawn Miller clutched her purse tightly to her quivering stomach and followed the personnel manager down a carpeted hall to the elevators.

With its polished marble, gleaming brass, and thick carpeting, the bank building didn't even remotely resemble her image of a dragon's lair. Yet, from her sister Lisa's description, Matt Ivans ate financial clerks for breakfast and spit them out before lunch.

However, her younger sister always did have an active imagination. Only three years separated them, but at twenty-four Dawn felt far older . . . and wiser.

Mrs. Stoddard pushed the button to call the elevator. "I'm certain you'll find working for Mr. Ivans just the challenge you're looking for, Ms. Miller," she said with a smile.

Dawn wished the woman had phrased it a little differently. In her present frame of mind, she didn't find that particular choice of words very reassuring. She managed a small smile in return, and answered, "I'm sure I will," before covertly checking her reflection in the polished brass doors.

Her honey-shaded hair remained immaculate in a classic French twist. Liner and shadow accented her brown eyes evenly and subtly. She ran a damp palm down her skirt, smoothing away nonexistent wrinkles.

The doors slid open and she followed the older woman into

1

a tastefully decorated elevator for the ride to the third floor. A moment later the doors rolled back to reveal a wide, bright room carpeted in the same deep mauve as the bank's main floor. Along one wall tall windows let in the mid-morning sun and provided a panoramic view of tree-shaded streets. A neighborhood of neatly landscaped homes edged the small suburban business district on Fort Worth's western edge, the soft green of tender growth a testament to spring's renewing power. A renewing Dawn desperately needed.

A maze of cubicles formed by fabric-covered panels created a puzzle board of sound and activity. Telephones rang, computers hummed, people scurried to and fro, and over it all droned the low buzz of human conversation. No, the cheerful melange didn't look anything at all like the hideout of a woman-eating dragon.

Mrs. Stoddard nodded to their left. "The automotive loan department is this way."

Dawn followed in her wake as she pointed out the restroom, break room, the fax machine, and then led her right up to Matt Ivans's desk to make the introductions.

The individual in question stood to greet them, towering over Dawn's five-feet, four-inch frame by a good ten inches. She had a quick impression of broad shoulders and thick black hair in the second before he spoke. Then her gaze locked with his.

"Ms. Miller," he acknowledged, his tone clipped. The silver-gray eyes were sharp and intelligent, his regard frankly assessing. Dawn had the distinct impression she didn't measure up.

"This is a busy department. I hope you're ready to jump in with both feet."

Responding to his challenge, she stood a little straighter and lifted her chin a notch, her gaze never wavering. "I'm not afraid of work, Mr. Ivans. You can rest assured I'll give you my best effort."

His eyes widened for a split-second in an expression of surprise, then narrowed as he arched one dark brow, pinning her in place with a hard-edged look. "I suppose that's all any-one can expect, isn't it?" he murmured, his voice a low growl.

The deep tone struck a forgotten chord somewhere in her soul and a chill skimmed down her arms. "Ye . . ." She swallowed and tried again, unable to break the hold of his piercing gaze. "Yes, I suppose it is."

Mrs. Stoddard spoke. "Ms. Miller trained for two hours this morning for your department, Mr. Ivans, and I must say she caught on very quickly to the forms and procedures."

"Glad to hear it, Mrs. Stoddard," the man replied, but Dawn could tell he wasn't all that convinced. What the heck was his problem anyway?

A strong hand, its back lightly dusted with black hair, lifted into her field of vision and indicated the other desk in the cubicle. "That's your spot. Put your things up and we'll get started."

Dawn tamped down her unexpected reaction and followed his brusque directive, suppressing the urge to respond with a salute and a crisp, "Yes sir!"

The man was all business. Good. Her startling response to him had to be nothing more than an aberration caused by first-day jitters. Heaven knew she was finished with emotional en-tanglements. Been there, done that. Never again. She would take care of herself from now on out, thank you very much.

She removed her suit jacket and hung it on the back of her chair. Mr. Ivans handed her a half dozen faxed loan requests and she took her seat. She'd finished processing three of them when she heard him thump his coffee mug down on his desk.

"Ms. Miller, see if you can improve on what's in the bottom of that coffeepot, would you?"

Dawn looked at him over her shoulder. Not a request, but an order. "Excuse me?"

"Coffee," he responded, the growl back in his voice. "Please make some fresh coffee." He paused, then asked, "You do know how, don't you?"

She hid a smirk and bit back a smart retort. It wouldn't do to be fired her first day on the job. Modulating her voice to cool professionalism, she replied, "I can probably figure it out, Mr. Ivans."

"Good. I take mine black. No sugar."

Just like his soul, she thought. "Yes, Mr. Ivans."

The making and serving of coffee certainly wasn't in her job description, but no big deal. The bank paid for her time and she had no problem with it.

Several minutes later, she placed the mug on a corner of his desk and pulled out her chair. Before she could sit down again he demanded, "Where are the faxes? Didn't you bring them back with you?"

"No, I'm sorry. I'll get them."

He canted sideways and frowned at her over his shoulder. "We have to keep up with those things; time is money in this department. If I don't get back to the car dealers right away, they'll look for someone else to buy the paper, and we lose the loan."

It was fortunate, Dawn thought with a sigh, that she wasn't as sensitive as she used to be. Obviously she'd need a pretty thick skin to get through the days with this man, but she could do it, she knew she could. She'd survived worse than a grumpy boss. The challenges to be found in the business world couldn't begin to compare with what she'd faced as a home-maker.

Once she'd retrieved the fax transmissions and settled into the rhythm of her work, what was left of the morning flew by. Mr. Ivans startled her when he announced, "You're missing lunch."

The break room was nearly deserted. Dawn tossed back a couple of aspirins to combat a tension headache and grimaced as she washed them down with a swallow of cola. She was unwrapping her cold beef sandwich when a diminutive blond entered and dropped into the seat beside her.

"Hi, I'm Mary. Your sister's told us a lot about you."

Dawn raised an eyebrow. "Oh?" The young woman looked to be about Lisa's age.

Mary giggled. "Yes, especially when she found out you got

the job with Mr. Ivans. Lisa said if anyone could tame him it would be her big sister."

"Did she now?"

"Oh, don't get me wrong, it's not like we gossiped about you or anything."

"Of course not."

"I know how it sounds, but it's just that most of us have worked for him at one time or another, and none of us lasted more than four weeks." The girl sighed. "I only lasted three days."

"What happened?"

"I ran off in tears. Three days of his snapping at me was all I could take. I think I hold the record for the shortest time."

"And the others?"

"Most just didn't want to deal with it. Some yelled back and then quit. One, a reserve deputy with the sheriff's office, told him where he could stuff his computer terminal right before she dumped his coffee in his lap. She didn't even bother to quit; she just never came back. He gets traffic tickets from the sheriff's department now." Mary snickered. "A lot of them."

Dawn shook her head in amazement. "If he has so much trouble keeping clerks, why does the bank keep him on?"

"He has the highest loan acquisition rate in this entire region."

"Ah, yes. Money. The bottom line. That would explain it, I suppose, but even with such a personnel turnover?"

Mary nodded. "Even with. He puts in a lot of hours."

"So there's no chink in the big man's armor, huh?"

"None that I know of . . . except for the fact that he hates strawberries. Really though, how are you doing with him?"

"Fine so far. However, if he starts breathing fire I may come looking for a safe place to hide."

Mary's eyes twinkled. "Come ahead, there's plenty of room under my desk. I'm on the second floor, section five."

"Great," Dawn replied with a roll of her eyes, but personally, she didn't understand all the fuss. Mr. Ivans was just a man. Unquestionably abrupt, but a man. No more, no less.

An hour after she returned from lunch, Dawn reached over to drop a batch of processed applications into her boss's IN basket just as he returned from a meeting. He nodded to her. She inclined her head slightly and said, "Good afternoon, Mr. Ivans," then turned back to her work without waiting for a reply.

"Matt."

"I'm sorry?" She wasn't certain she'd heard him speak.

"Call me Matt."

"As you wish." She returned her attention to her job. Out of the corner of her eye she saw him frown and smiled to herself. If he wanted conversation out of her, he'd have to work a little harder for it than that.

The remainder of the day passed quickly with no major snags and her confidence grew in proportion to the number of applications processed. With a smile of satisfaction, she covered her computer terminal at the end of the day.

"So, what did you think of Ivans the Terrible?"

Dawn shot her younger sister a disgusted look. "What *I* think, is that you're too easily intimidated."

"Hoo boy," Lisa crowed, "I can see the fur flying already. I knew you'd be the perfect match for him." Rubbing her hands together gleefully she added, "I can't wait."

Dawn shook her head and went to her bedroom to change out of her suit. What *did* she think of Mr. Ivans? *Matt?* Dropping to the edge of the bed and pulling off one high-heeled pump, she reviewed her first day with her new boss.

A fine figure of a man, as the saying went, he was also handsome, she'd grant him that. Not that she cared, she really didn't, but a woman would have to be comatose not to notice those silvery eyes, contrasting as they did with thick black hair and sable lashes. She supposed his looks would best be described as rugged. Yes, definitely rugged. Matt Ivans was a handsome, rugged, virile male. So what.

But that voice. Thinking of the way his tone dropped to a low rumbling growl when he was displeased, the chill returned to run down her spine and she shivered, then ruthlessly tamped down the unwanted sensation.

Struggling to maintain her objectivity, she considered his behavior, his brusque manner of communication. Matt Ivans wasn't exactly what one would call a people person. She supposed that accounted for his nickname, but though she'd found him terse and maybe grumpy, she didn't think him terrible.

Pulling herself from her reverie, she finished changing clothes and emerged a few minutes later barefooted, in shorts and a T-shirt, finger-combing her shoulder-length hair.

After dinner, Dawn took a glass of iced tea out on the balcony while Lisa showered. She drew in a deep breath of the cooling evening air, and leaned her elbows on the railing as she studied the nearly level landscape spread before her. Against the eastern horizon the skyline of Fort Worth sat like a contractor's model on a flat table. The fading spring twilight painted the buildings a smoky blue, their details indistinct at this distance.

Ahead of her to the north, the runway lights of Carswell Military Base twinkled like grounded stars, while to the west, the last vestiges of daylight stained the scattered clouds an improbable shade of pink.

She took a long sip of her drink then pulled up a folding lawn chair and sat. Lifting her legs, she propped her heels on the wrought-iron rail. Today had not only been the first in her new job but the first, really, in her new life. When she'd moved from the Houston area a week ago, she'd left behind a two-year nightmare of excruciating emotional pain and heartbreak. She'd left behind a failed marriage—and all but the memories of her precious child.

This job was nothing spectacular, just an entry-level post in the automotive loan department of StarAmerica Bank, where Lisa also worked, but it was a start. And she needed a new start. Sweet Heaven, how she needed a new start.

Matt Ivans hung up the telephone, leaned his elbows on his desk, and massaged the back of his neck. What a job for a grown man, pushing paper all day long so some poor soul could spend the next five years of his life paying for a pickup truck.

He sighed and stretched. He was good at it though, and the work paid decently. Coupled with his military disability it gave him a tidy income, but he felt out of his depth working with so many females. He'd much rather be back leading a squad of men.

As an Army helicopter pilot, his talent for whipping a crew of self-centered boys into a unit of responsible men had far outweighed his skill in dealing with a gaggle of emotional women. You never knew what might set one of them off. They'd either run out bawling over nothing, or snap his head off over some little thing, then quit. Go figure.

Maybe this new one would be different. She'd only started yesterday, but seemed pretty sharp, picking up quickly on the procedures, as promised. She was easy on the eye, too, and judging from the way she had of standing her ground, he didn't think she'd be the kind to dissolve into tears at the drop of a hat.

The sharp report of high heels striking the tile-floored main aisle alerted him to her approach. With a swish of soft fabric and the faint hint of honeysuckle, his newest clerk appeared at his side and wished him a good morning.

Soft fabric? Honeysuckle?

As she stored her purse and turned her computer terminal on, he watched her covertly. The nearby fax machine beeped the arrival of loan requests, reminding him to get back to work.

She took away his empty coffee cup and he raised his head to watch her go, the floral scent trailing in her wake. What was her name? He'd gone through so many recently.

He grabbed up a processed form, but it only bore her initials, DLM. Then it came to him: Miller. Her last name was Miller, but he couldn't remember any more. She set the cup of steaming coffee at his side, and he leaned back in his chair, nodded, and said pleasantly, "Thank you, Miller."

"You're welcome, Mr. Ivans."

He frowned. "I told you to call me Matt."

She seated herself at her desk and began to flip through the stack of transmissions as she answered, "Ah, yes. Then would you mind terribly calling me either Ms. Miller, or Dawn? It makes me feel like a construction hand to be called just Miller."

His eyebrows shot up. "Dawn? You don't look like a Dawn."

The hint of a smile played at one corner of her mouth. "Well, what can I say? My parents were products of the sixties. I'm lucky it wasn't Starlight or Moonbeam."

He chuckled. "Yeah, I guess you are at that. No offense intended. Dawn it is."

Had she imagined that edge in his laugh? His expression seemed bland enough, but Dawn couldn't help feeling that Mr. Ivans didn't care to be corrected, even when he was wrong. Maybe *especially* when he was wrong.

She returned from lunch that afternoon to find her boss still on the telephone. She'd nearly finished an application when he hung up, another deal completed.

"I'm snowed under today, Dawn. Run down to the corner and get me a double cheeseburger, large fries, and a milkshake." He tossed a ten-dollar bill onto her desk.

Gritting her teeth, she nodded. In order to "run down to the corner" she'd have to get the car keys from Lisa because she sure didn't intend to scurry to the far end of the block and back in high heels.

By the time she left Lisa's office, she'd reached the conclusion that this might be a test. Of course. She'd confronted him this morning over his brusque greeting, and this was his reparation. A wicked little smile tilted her lips. No problem, she could handle it.

"Here you are, Matt. All nice and hot."

He grunted his thanks, only to gasp a few minutes later, "Strawberry! You got me a strawberry milkshake?"

"You don't like strawberry?" Voice laced with deep concern, Dawn opened her eyes wide in her best parody of innocence. "I'm sorry. You didn't tell me what flavor you wanted, so I picked my favorite. Would you like something from the drink machine?"

"No," he grouched, reaching into his desk drawer. "Just take the shake and get me a cup of coffee."

"Yes, sir," she answered, careful to keep her tone contrite as she hopped up to do his bidding.

"I could swear she did it on purpose," Matt fumed that weekend.

"Matthew, why would she do a thing like that? I don't think she'd want to jeopardize her job. You admitted you forgot to tell her what kind of shake to get." His mother paused for a moment. "Besides," she asked slowly, "why did you send her out to get your lunch in the first place?"

He didn't meet his mother's eyes. "I, ah, was really busy and didn't want to take time out for lunch, so I asked her to get it for me."

"Matthew." His mother's warning tone made him feel ten years old.

"Oh, all right! We'd had a little verbal sparring match earlier and I wanted to establish just who was in charge."

"Oh, Matthew." She sighed, shaking her head.

"I know, pretty childish, huh?"

"To say the least. I can't believe that any son of your father's is so inept at dealing with women. You're thirty-two, not twelve, you know."

He grunted in disgust. "Dad has a nice, normal woman to deal with. I'd like to see how he'd do with an office full of career women."

His mother laughed and shook her head. "Where did I go wrong?"

He was uneasy with this conversation. Having only brothers, and all of them older, he'd grown up in a household of men, overseen by his decidedly domestic mother. Maybe that's why his attitudes fit more comfortably in a previous age.

He believed women should stay home, cook, and be mothers, as his own mother had. Just as he believed that men should be strong, protective, and independent.

He'd been content in the Army. He could live a man's life as he saw it and only occasionally have to contend with women who didn't fit his mold. If only Sgt. Smith had stayed home with her two young sons, she would still be alive. Mothers didn't belong in the Army, they belonged at home!

Their helicopter had malfunctioned during maneuvers. He'd been unable to control the descent and the crash that mangled his leg had killed his female crew chief, the only woman on board. For months afterwards, nightmares shattered his rest. He'd wake himself and his parents with his moans. The pain. His injured crew. Sgt. Smith. Matt shook his head to dispel the memories.

That night, he lay in his old room with his hands folded behind his head, and stared at the ceiling, wondering why he'd come back to the home place this weekend.

He only flew up to his folks' for holidays, or when troubled, or needing a break. Well, heck, with the long hours he'd been putting in, he certainly deserved the break.

Contending with his new clerk left him pretty wired, too. He had no idea how long this one would last, or even if he wanted her to.

Strawberry, for Pete's sake! She might have killed him. No, to be truthful, at the very worst, he broke out in a rash. An irritating, itchy rash, but not hives. He hadn't even known he had this allergy until the company picnic last summer.

His new clerk. *Dawn.* A woman as fresh and cool as her name. She hadn't cried or raised her voice all week, but she was no mouse either. He chuckled to himself. More than once he'd seen the flash of fire in those doe-brown eyes . . . like when he'd sent her after his lunch. No, she had plenty of spirit hidden under that professional exterior. He doubted she went home at night to sob into her pillow.

He peered into the dark and wondered idly whether someone shared that pillow with her, then found his thoughts drifting to honey-gold hair spread across crisp linen, soft lips parted for kissing.

"Forget it, Ivans," he growled to the empty room. "She's a *career woman.*"

Chapter Two

Monday morning Matt slapped the chart of the previous week's figures down in front of Dawn. "Our productivity is down. We've slipped to second place."

Dawn flinched when he hit her desk, but was determined he not see that he'd startled her. It hadn't taken her long to recognize his competitive spirit, and she realized his foul mood was prompted by frustration.

"Matt," she responded, "I'm learning as fast as I can. Perhaps if you brought your lunch, we could get back up there again."

Confusion flashed in his eyes, only to turn to suspicion. "Brought my lunch?"

"Yes," she replied sweetly, "then I could do my job here, instead of running down to the corner for hamburgers."

A scowl drew his brows together and a flush started up his neck. Grumbling under his breath, he turned sharply and threw himself into his chair. "Do you best," he muttered over his shoulder.

"Yes, sir."

She heard him call personnel for a floater to help her catch up with his accounts. It had been a busy weekend for car sales, and the applications were stacked several inches deep.

An hour later a young woman dropped a sheaf of applications in his box, then paused at Dawn's desk. "Hi, I'm Lilly.

Don't worry, we'll have him caught up in no time." She waggled two fingers and departed in a cloud of noxious perfume. Dawn stared after the girl a moment, then shook her head and returned to her work.

From his desk, Matt hid a grin. His reaction to Lilly was exactly the same. Black hair streaked orange, and cracking gum—not his idea of the perfect assistant, and never mind earrings the size of hubcaps and a knit skirt three sizes too small. She must be someone's relative to get away with flouting the dress code the way she did. Involuntarily, his gaze drifted to Dawn. Much nicer, he thought, before catching himself.

Late the in the afternoon he erupted again. "Dawn! How can I process an application without a complete address? What's with this generic Zip code? You know the addresses have to be exact," he challenged through gritted teeth.

She reached for the offending form. She didn't recall this one, but quickly looked up the Zip code and corrected it.

Not fifteen minutes later, he shot out of his chair as though spring-loaded. "Confound it, the credit bureau kicked this one back because the Social Security number doesn't match the name. You're costing me time and money." He shook the sheet of paper in the air. "If you aren't suited to a career, stay home and have babies."

Dawn gasped. This time he'd cut her. Really cut deep. She wanted to scream at him that she'd love to do just that, but the choice wasn't hers!

Reaching out a trembling hand, she retrieved the deficient form. Sure enough, in transferring from the fax copy to the computer form, the middle two digits had been transposed. Matt returned to his desk with a disgusted grunt.

Dawn's eyes dropped to the corner box. LPF. Those weren't her initials. Lilly had prepared this one. Angrily, she grabbed up a highlighter and circled the box, then threw the paper down in front of Matt.

Without glancing at her notation, he jumped to his feet. Hands on his hips, he glowered down at her. "Dawn" he began. His voice, low and menacing, rolled like ominous thunder. "I don't think you realize your position here. You're still a probationary employee. You'd better get with the program and fast," he growled. "You're a smart lady. I don't think I have to spell out the worst-case scenario for you, do I?"

She mirrored his stance, her head thrown back to meet his glare, and gave him a short, dry laugh. "Mister, I have survived the *mother* of worst-case scenarios, and you don't even place a distant second!"

Dawn's pulse pounded furiously in her ears as she snatched up her purse and jacket. Matt caught her arm as she pushed past him, but released it when she looked pointedly at his hand.

"Where are you going?" he demanded.

She trembled in her fury. "To lunch," she snapped. "Would you like a milkshake?"

He retreated a step, running a hand through his thick dark hair. "No, thanks," he retorted. "You'd probably put hemlock in it this time."

"Darn straight," she gritted, then pivoted on her heel and stalked from the cubicle.

Matt watched her go, then dropped heavily into his chair. He cursed softly and drew both palms down his face.

Dawn peeled out of the parking lot with a screech of tires. Several blocks away, she pulled into a small park and under the wide spreading limbs of an ancient oak tree. Hands curled over the top of the steering wheel, she dropped her forehead to her knuckles and let the pain take her. *Stay home and have babies!*

Grief broke over her in waves. Building, building, until it threatened to drown her. She drew in a shuddering breath and the tidal wave of emotion pulled her under. She began to cry.

And cry.

And cry.

Great choking sobs racked her slender body, shaking the very core of her being, draining her strength, destroying her control. She cried as she'd never cried before, giving vent to all the pain, all the sorrow of the last several months. Grieving for all she'd lost, all she'd never have again.

When she finally leaned her head back on the seat, her eyes actually hurt from so much weeping. She didn't care if he fired her, the colossal jerk. She could always find another job. It was what he'd said about staying home with babies that devastated her. Three years ago she'd been doing just that.

Her job at StarAmerica was her first position since getting her life back on track, but she really had no concern about losing it. Like she'd told that Neanderthal: in the face of real tragedy, losing a job didn't even rate.

Matt kept checking his watch. Was the blasted thing even running? Surely she'd been gone more than a half hour? His work lay forgotten. Every time someone approached his area, he looked up, expecting to see her.

No, not really. Recalling the stricken expression, her pale face, he never expected to see her again. Still, he looked up hoping to find her there. Forty-five minutes. She'd been gone forty-five minutes now.

Wiping her face dry, Dawn blew her nose and closed her eyes wearily. What time had she left the office? It didn't matter. She'd go back when she was good and ready. If she even went back at all.

She started the car and drove to a nearby Mexican restaurant. Before taking a seat in the quaint little eatery, she went to the ladies' room to repair her makeup. She splashed her face with cold water and patted it dry with paper towels. Staring at her reflection in the mirror, she realized there wasn't much she could do for her red puffy eyes but wait for the swelling to go down.

What now? You've just blown your new job.

Maybe, maybe not.

Fishing in her purse for a brush, Dawn tidied her hair. The woman looking back from the glass needed more to put her back together than these few cosmetic repairs.

He was the one in the wrong, whether or not he cares to

16 *Cheri Jetton*

admit it. So he got to you—that doesn't mean you have to chuck it all and slink away. You're made of stronger stuff than that! She tossed her brush back into her purse and strode from the restroom.

In a fit of rebellion, she ordered a large frozen margarita to go with her chicken chimichanga with sour cream and guacamole. The waitress, a plump, middle-aged woman, studied her face a moment, then went off muttering, *"¡Hombres! ¡Todos es malos!"*

When the waitress returned with the frosty drink, she also handed Dawn two ice cubes in small plastic bags. "For your eyes. You don' want him to know he make you cry."

Dawn smiled up at her. "No, I sure don't. Thank you."

An hour and fifty minutes after leaving, she walked purposefully back to her desk, smacked a chocolate milkshake down by Matt's elbow, put her purse away, and went back to work, all without a word.

Neither spoke for the remainder of the day, but Dawn noticed that he drank the milkshake. He probably thought of it as a peace offering instead of what it really represented—a dare.

Quitting time. Dawn arched her back, then rotated her head to work the kinks out of her neck. After straightening her desk, she glanced over at Matt's square shoulders, started to say good night, thought better of it, and turned away with a tired sigh.

"Dawn?" His voice was low but quiet.

She paused.

He'd swiveled to face her, one ankle propped on the opposite knee. "Would you be able to come in a little early tomorrow? I could use your help to catch up." He plowed one hand through his hair. "Many of the preliminaries that Lilly did are incomplete. You know, missing data, incorrect addresses, that sort of thing."

She studied him for a moment. This was probably as close to an apology as the man had ever come.

"Of course, Mr. Ivans."

"Matt," he corrected softly.

She nodded and turned away again.

"Dawn?"

Now what? She looked at him over her shoulder.

"Thank you for the milkshake."

"Hey," Lisa greeted as she climbed into the car. "I hear the feathers hit the fan today. Are you okay?"

"Bloodied and bowed, but unbroken."

"No kidding, Dawn, are you all right?"

Dawn spared a quick glance for her sister as she pulled into the evening traffic. "It got pretty rough, but I'll make it. Or kill him trying."

"That's more like it. I heard you two were nose to nose, but no one seemed to know why."

"He gave me heat for his productivity being down." Dawn snorted. "He sends me out for his lunch, they give him a floater who can't process an application to save her life, and he comes down on me."

"What did he say?"

"Something about worst-case scenarios and staying home with babies if I couldn't do the job."

Lisa gasped, her expression stricken. "Oh, Dawn, I'm so sorry. It's all my fault, I shouldn't have gotten you into this."

"None of it's your fault. He had no idea he'd hit a nerve. I don't think even Ivans would be that cold. At least I hope not."

"No, I'm sure you're right," the younger woman conceded softly. "So what did you say to him before you took off for your extended lunch?"

Dawn raised an eyebrow in her sister's direction. "My, the gossip mill doesn't miss a thing, does it?"

Lisa shrugged.

"I told him I'd already survived the mother of worst-case scenarios and he didn't even rate second place."

"You didn't!" Lisa gasped. Then her eyes lit with glee. "You did, I know you did!" she crowed. "Fantastic! What now?"

"He wants me to come in early tomorrow to help catch up. Do you want to drive yourself or come in with me?"

"You mean you're going to do it? He sits on his haunches all afternoon looking at his watch, then expects you to help him make it up?"

"He asked me, very nicely, so I agreed. What do you mean about his watch?"

"Word has it that after you left he did almost nothing. He answered incoming calls, but didn't call out to any of his accounts, and he kept looking at his watch. He didn't get back into sync until you showed up again. Interesting, huh?"

"Very."

"You say he *asked* you to come in? Not ordered?"

"That's right, asked. And very politely, too."

"I don't believe for a minute that the battle's over, but I think you're ahead on points," Lisa pronounced smugly.

"Yeah, right." To herself Dawn thought, if this is how it felt to be ahead, she'd never survive a defeat.

Matt glanced up at Dawn's approach, an hour early as promised. "We need to talk," he said.

He heard her draw in a deep breath as she straightened her small frame to its erect limits. "Yes, Mr. Ivans?"

He let it pass this time and watched her steel herself as though bracing for an attack. She stood straight and proud, but defensive. Just like a soldier on the line.

Maybe that's how she felt, he thought. Maybe he made everyone feel that way, like soldiers going into combat. Could he really be that awful?

"I owe you an apology." He dropped his gaze to his hands. "I acted like a madman yesterday, blaming you for things that weren't your fault."

He glanced up expecting to meet an icy stare, but found instead eyes dulled by pain. The only light evident in the rich brown irises was that provided by unshed tears. Blast! He swallowed. "I said some very stupid things," he admitted as he again dropped his gaze.

Her eyes had haunted him through the long night. The

shock and pain they'd registered when he'd told her to stay home if she couldn't handle the job were a sharp jab to his conscience. He didn't want to witness again the suffering that had snuffed their lively sparkle.

But he had to, she deserved it. He had to be looking her straight in the eye when he said it. Sighing, he stood. "Dawn, I'm sorry. I hope you can forgive me."

The naked pain in her gaze made him flinch. For the life of him, he would never knowingly hurt a woman. Especially not one as delicate of frame and strong of spirit as this one. This awful moment would stay with him forever . . . right next to the memory of Sgt. Smith's broken body hanging out the door of a smashed helicopter.

Why didn't women stay home where they'd be safe? Why did they have to have such tender feelings? All he'd done was yell a little, for Pete's sake!

Yesterday when she'd been gone so long, he'd given up hoping she'd return. Meeting her gaze now, he almost wished she hadn't.

Dawn swallowed against the pressure in her chest and studied Matt's troubled face. That he truly regretted his outburst was unimpeachable. He cleared his throat and she realized he waited for a response.

"You weren't that terrible," she murmured, "you just hit a nerve is all. I can forget it if you can."

"I don't want to forget it," he argued, his voice a little rough. "If I did, there might be a repeat, and I don't want that. Not ever. I want us to try to get past it, to work around it, but I can't let myself forget."

"Fair enough. We'll make a new start as of this morning, okay?" she offered quietly.

Matt smiled at her, a tentative lifting of those full lips, and she smiled back.

As the office filled, Dawn ignored the many speculative looks directed their way, working diligently on reducing the pile of applications on her desk. They'd been hard at it for nearly five hours when she stood to stretch her cramped muscles, groaning slightly as she did so.

Matt looked over his shoulder as she massaged her neck and rolled her head. "Go take your lunch break. I've got plenty to work on until you get back," he directed.

"If it's okay with you, I can eat my sandwich while I work. I think we can get most of it caught up if I do that and we stay an extra hour tonight."

"Okay, but get up and walk around once in a while, or you won't be able to stand straight tomorrow."

"Good idea."

Matt glanced up when she returned with her lunch and set a chilled can of cola at his elbow. He couldn't decide whether to be pleased or annoyed. He'd behaved abominably, yet she was willing to overlook it . . . after having had her say, of course. A smile tugged at the corner of his mouth. She really might work out after all.

Some time later, he heard a soft sound and turned in his chair. "How are you doing?"

"I'm getting there." She sighed, rotating her shoulders. "If we aren't totally caught up by the time we leave tonight, we won't be far from it."

"No, I meant you personally. How are you holding up? You can knock off if you want."

"I'll make it. I really would like to get this backlog cleared up."

He nodded. "Okay, thanks. I owe you."

She muttered, "You've got that right," and he shot her a look over his shoulder. She returned the look with one eyebrow raised, as though daring him to dispute her.

"Are you going home for Easter?" Lisa asked from the kitchen where she scrubbed the countertops. Saturdays they cleaned the apartment.

"I hadn't planned on it, why?"

"I don't know. Just that it's your first holiday away from home, is all."

Dawn laughed. "I don't think Dad hides eggs anymore, Lissy."

Lisa chuckled. "True. He says we're too big and the grandkids should hunt eggs at their own houses. I don't think he really liked playing Easter Bunny."

"Besides, if you want an Easter dinner, we can do our own here. Or do you have other plans?"

Lisa glanced over at her uncertainly. "Well, I do have an invitation, but I haven't committed myself. We can do a dinner here if you want; that would be great."

Dawn stopped dusting the coffee table and straightened, hands on her hips, to confront her little sister. "Lisa, I do not need a keeper. I'm grown up now, older than you even. What is the big deal here?"

"Like I said, it's your first time away from the folks."

"I have been 'away from the folks' since I married. I'm fine, really. If you're going to smother me with maternal concern, I'll have to find my own place."

"Sorry. I only wanted to help."

"I know, and I love you for it, but cut the protective bit, okay?"

Lisa grinned. "Okay. You won't mind if I go to church with Doug, then to dinner at his mom's?"

"Of course not! Now finish that kitchen so we can go to the mall."

Later, as Lisa shopped for a new outfit to wear Easter Sunday, Dawn looked just for the fun of it. She had plenty of clothes for work and little life outside the office, so she didn't need anything new. Still, a frothy little dress caught her eye, a floral-printed georgette, sleeveless, with a very full skirt.

Lisa saw her fingering the garment and urged, "Try it on."

"I don't need a new dress," she protested as she lifted the side of the skirt, fanning out yards of material.

"You need that one. 'Hyacinths for the soul', and all that."

Dawn smiled at the feminine confection. "Maybe you're right. Okay, I'll try it on, but it'll probably look silly on me."

Several words would serve to describe how the dress looked on her, Dawn thought; soft, airy, feminine, beguiling, maybe even sassy. Silly, however, was not one of them.

At home, she admired the dress anew and mused, "I don't

know why I bought this. I can't think when I'll wear it; it would never do for the office."

"Maybe not, but I'm sure we'll find you a chance to show it off," Lisa assured her. "Doug is already bugging me for your social schedule. He has a couple of cousins and several friends who are anxious to meet you."

"Lisa." Dawn's voice held a warning note.

"I know, I know. I've told him you aren't interested, but he thinks you're great and can't stand to see you 'going to waste,' as he puts it. He sees some of the girls his friends show up with and it drives him crazy knowing there is an intelligent, attractive woman sitting at home in the evenings."

Dawn laughed. "Aren't you laying it on a bit thick?"

"Nope." Lisa raised one hand, palm out in pledge. "Those were his words. Honest."

Dawn shook her head and carried the new dress to her closet. As she hung it up, she smiled in spite of herself. It really did make her happy just looking at it.

The telephone rang in the next room and in a moment Lisa called out, "Dawn? Doug's on the phone. Ross Tudor is singing at the Old Oak Corral tonight and he'd like to take us. How about it?"

Dawn stuck her head out of her bedroom door and made a face at her sister while shaking her head.

Lisa covered the mouthpiece of the phone and pleaded, "Please, Dawn? You could wear your new dress, I'll wear a dress too. Or if you want, we can wear jeans. Please?"

"You can go without me," Dawn insisted. "It's not like he's going to withdraw the invitation if I don't go."

"I know, but I'd really like for you to come with us. They say Ross is the next Clint Black, and besides, you need to live a little."

Dawn sighed in defeat. "All right. But make sure he understands I don't intend to make a habit of this." She knew without a doubt they'd be joined by one of Doug's friends.

The rustic tavern sat on the outskirts of Fort Worth's historical stockyard district. Low-ceilinged and dimly lit, it had a smooth plank bar that ran down the right-hand wall. Oak barstools, covered in red vinyl and studded with brass nails, stood sentinel along the length of highly polished wood.

Neon beer signs adorned three walls of the club, casting a muted, multicolored glow. Behind the bar, an expanse of mirrors reflected and magnified the room's sparse lighting.

"Doug, Lisa, over here." A stocky man in a black cowboy hat gestured to them from a cluster of tables near the stage. At this early hour, there weren't too many people in the place, but it looked to Dawn as if Doug's friends had filled the three tables at center stage.

Worse than she expected, out of the nine people waiting for them, only three were women. That left three men who were probably here to check her out. She gave her sister a withering glare. Lisa shrugged and looked to Doug who seemed as bewildered as she.

Doug cleared his throat and performed the introductions. "Everybody, this is Lisa's sister, Dawn Miller. Dawn, this is everybody."

Hoots and jeers filled the air. Someone complained, "Come on now, Doug, do it right. I didn't break my neck getting over here to remain anonymous."

The man who'd hailed them stood, removed his hat as he pulled out the chair beside him, and took Dawn's elbow. "It's a pleasure to meet you, Dawn. I'm Jerry. Doug and I were college roommates. The sore loser there"—he pointed his hat at the young man who had complained—"is his cousin Sam. Next to him is Billy Johnson, John Lowden, and Mary Sills. At the far table is Bev Willis, Mark Duncan, Sarah Morris, and Mike Hernandez. We are all pleased to meet you, as Lisa has spoken of you often," he finished formally, and guided her into the chair.

Dawn sat facing the other tables, and couldn't help feeling like a scientific specimen under a microscope. When their beverages were ordered, Doug asked for dinner menus, explaining, "There isn't much of a choice, but what they do have is great."

The menu, indeed sparse, offered only chili in three different forms, and four different cuts of beefsteak. The steaks came with salad and a choice of fries or a baked potato.

"I'd suggest the rib-eye," offered Jerry, "and the baked potato if you like them. They come dressed with all the trimmings here."

Dawn smiled at him, and said, "Sounds good to me. Rib-eye, medium, and baked potato with all the goodies."

Jerry nodded and gave their orders to the waitress. Jerry was a little older than Doug and the others, and Dawn liked the way he took command without being pushy.

Their dinner orders placed, Doug leaned back in his chair so he could see Sam at the next table and asked, "I thought you had to work tonight?"

"I did, but when I heard that Dawn might finally make an appearance I swapped hours with someone." He glared at Jerry.

Jerry saluted him with his beer bottle and teased, "Better luck next time."

Doug looked at Billy. "You alone tonight too?"

Billy, at least, had the grace to look embarrassed. "Yep." He didn't say anything more, but looked at Dawn and smiled shyly. She was mortified. She'd strangle Lisa when they got home. If she could wait that long!

Jerry patted her hand. "Don't look so miserable. We aren't going to cut you up into shares, but you can't blame us for being curious. You are all Lisa has talked about ever since she found out you'd be moving up here with her. And Doug has sung your praises loud and long as well.

"From what I've heard, though," he continued, lowering his voice, "you're too smart for Billy to be comfortable with, and Sam will be too immature for you. So you see, it's really not a problem."

Dawn eyed him skeptically. "And what about you?"

He smiled, his eyes twinkling as he pushed his hat to the back of his head with one finger under the front brim. "Well, ma'am," he drawled, "I'm hoping to be the lucky one."

The club filled while they ate their dinner, then someone put a slow song on the jukebox and Jerry stood, pulling her to her feet. "Come on, you have to start out slow after eating a big meal."

Dawn tugged her fingers from his grasp and asked sweetly, one eyebrow raised in censure, "Does that translate to 'may I have this dance'?"

A slow grin climbed one side of his deeply tanned face as he swept his hat from his head and bowed low. "Ms. Miller, may I have the pleasure of this dance?"

Her eyebrow still cocked, Dawn replied, "That's better." Then she added imperiously, "I'd be delighted, sir."

Jerry began laughing before he'd even straightened and continued to chuckle as he took her elbow and led her onto the dance floor.

"Ms. Miller, I do believe you're going to lead me on one merry chase," he observed as he swung her into his arms.

Settling against him as he began moving her to the slow strains of Reba McEntire's "You Lied," Dawn looked up into his laughing eyes and informed him serenely, "You may call me Dawn, and there won't be any chase. I won't be running. I'm not available for pursuit."

"Oh, really?"

"Yes, really."

He pulled her closer, tucking her head under his jaw, and murmured, "We'll see about that."

Chapter Three

The other men claimed dances with Dawn. Sam led her around the floor in a lively two-step, and Billy gazed soulfully at her during a slow number, before Jerry cut in. When she sat down again, she found herself the only woman at the table with her three admirers, but she'd begun to relax and took it in stride, spreading her attention among them.

Actually, it made things easier. With all three of them at the same table, the mood remained light and playful so that no one became seriously aggressive. They took turns dancing with her, claiming dances ahead of time in good-natured rivalry, and she teased with them as a group, feeling much like the adult counselor at a boys' camp.

Soon Ross would come on stage for his performance, and Jerry had claimed this slow dance. The crowd now filled the club nearly to capacity, and the dance floor was jammed.

"Are you having a good time?" he asked.

"Yes, I am."

"You sound surprised. Didn't you expect to?"

"Not really. I didn't want to be put on display as Lisa's big sister. I felt like the new attraction at the zoo."

He laughed and swung her in a circle.

"Also, I'm content with keeping to myself," she continued. "I'm not looking for anyone and I don't want anyone pestering

26

me, so you can imagine how it felt to come in here and have three of you waiting to pass judgment."

"Pass judgment? Is that how you felt?"

She nodded against his shoulder.

"Ready to pounce on you, maybe, but we're the ones who expected to be judged. In case you haven't noticed, we're still competing for your approval."

Dawn drew back so she could look up at him. He appeared totally serious. The song ended and she let the conversation drop.

As Dawn returned with Lisa from a trip to the ladies' room a short while later, a deep voice from the bar stopped her.

"Hello, Dawn."

The familiar low tones rolled up her spine and down again, stopping her in her tracks. She peered at the man sitting half turned, one elbow resting on the surface behind him.

"Matt?"

He stood, his silver-eyed gaze steady on her. Momentarily speechless, she stared back, then started when Lisa nudged her in the ribs.

"Oh! Ah, Mr. Ivans, I'd like you to meet my sister, Lisa. She works in Accounts Receivable. Lisa, I believe you know who Mr. Ivans is."

"Lisa," he acknowledged, casting her only the briefest glance.

"Of course I know who Mr. Ivans is," Lisa answered sweetly. "I'm so glad Dawn's working for you. I'll see you at the table, Sis."

Traitor, Dawn thought as Lisa quickly moved away, leaving her alone with Matt. Well, not exactly alone; there were close to three hundred people in the room, but at the moment she saw no one else, snared as she was by his gaze.

"Would you like a drink?"

"Thanks, but my, ah, friends are waiting for me." She had trouble breaking the imprisoning eye contact.

"Yes, I've noticed you have quite a fan club over there." His voice, low and intimate, brushed her like roughened velvet.

"Um," she stammered again, "actually, they're Lisa's friends. And her boyfriend, and his cousins."

"But it looks like you're the main attraction for tonight," he observed dryly.

She chuckled. "Something like that."

"Well, if you're doing your community service, might I have a dance, too?"

Dawn lifted startled eyes to Matt's face just as Jerry approached and took her arm. "Dawn, I thought the girls had misplaced you," he said pleasantly while giving Ivans a look that was anything but.

"Matt, this is Jerry Stevens. Jerry, this is Mr. Ivans, my boss."

The men didn't shake hands but only nodded as they sized each other up. They were of a height, a couple of inches over six feet. And both were solidly built, although Matt's conditioning wasn't as obvious. Jerry, on the other hand, worked in the construction trade and his beefy arms and barrel chest would be impossible to hide.

Dawn didn't like the tension that crackled in the building silence, and laid a hand on Jerry's arm. "Mr. Ivans has just asked me for a dance, Jerry. I'll join you in a few minutes?"

"Okay. I'll wait for you here and save Mr. Ivans's stool for him," he agreed coolly.

A slight frown lined Matt's forehead and he started to speak, but Dawn took his arm and smiled up at him. "Shall we, Mr. Ivans?"

His glare shifted from Jerry to her as he allowed himself to be lead away. "Matt," he growled.

"I know," she acknowledged as she turned into his arms, "but I don't know Jerry very well, and he looked like he wanted to start a fight."

"Is he your date?"

"Sort of. Evidently he's the one I'm supposed to be fixed up with this evening. No one told me anything about it, of course."

He seemed to relax and pulled her a little closer. They

moved slowly around the floor in silence for a while before he pulled away enough to look down at her.

"You look very nice tonight."

"Thank you, kind sir."

"I like that dress."

"Me too, I just got it. Lisa talked me into it."

"Oh? Why'd she have to do that?"

"Well, it's not really appropriate for the office, and I don't go out much, so I didn't really need another dress. She insisted I get it as a morale booster."

"I see. Did it work?"

She smiled. "Yes, as a matter of fact."

"Good." He settled her against him again, only to pull back a moment later. "Why did your morale need boosting?"

Dawn cocked her brow and gave him a look that said, *Oh, come on!* Aloud, she replied, "No big deal, just a rough week at the office."

She could have sworn she saw a quick flush of color darken her boss's face before he pulled her to him this time. She smiled to herself when he rested his jaw against her forehead.

He danced simply, with slow gliding steps that were ridiculously easy to follow, but while dancing with Matt offered no challenge, she found it pleasantly relaxing. Besides, it gave her a chance to notice other things, like the firmness of the shoulder under her fingers, the warmth of the hand on her back, the spicy masculine scent of him. Being held in Matt Ivans's arms was comforting, comfortable. Too comfortable.

The music ended with them on the opposite side of the floor from where Jerry waited. Matt took his time walking her back through the crowd to the bar, a hand on her waist. Just before they reached Jerry, he thanked her for the dance, then added without smiling, "And Dawn? You can wear that dress to work anytime you want."

Sunday afternoon, Dawn sorted her laundry to the accompaniment of a country music station and thoughts of Matt Ivans. What had prompted him to ask her for a dance? Though he was not a great dancer, it had been more than pleasant moving across the floor in his embrace, seeing a side of him that she'd previously not been privy to.

Lisa called from the living room. "Dawn, telephone."

Could it be Matt? She hurried to answer.

"Hi, beautiful. How about a trip to the zoo? The weather's perfect."

She laughed, stifling a small twinge of disappointment. "Thanks, Jerry, but after last night I have too much empathy for the creatures on display. I don't think I'll ever enjoy a zoo again."

He laughed. "Then how about Six Flags? They've got a great roller coaster."

"It's tempting," she lied, "but I really need to get my laundry done."

"Okay, how about a quick hamburger at The Grill?"

"Sorry, not this time."

Jerry's voice dropped an octave as he asked, "Are you already involved with your boss?"

"Of course not."

"Then what? I didn't step on your toes, or wipe my hands on the tablecloth, or get drunk, or start any fights."

She couldn't help laughing, remembering the small polished wood tables. "There weren't any tablecloths."

"Well, if there had been, I still wouldn't have done it."

"I know, but I have chores to do. Lisa and I went shopping yesterday afternoon, so I didn't get finished. I'm sorry."

A heavy sigh hissed through the phone line. "Okay. What about next week? How about dinner and a movie Friday night?"

"Jerry, I've told you. I'm not—"

"I know, I know. So you've told me and I know you're not interested in a relationship. Now that's out of the way, can we just go out sometime and have a little fun together?"

Why not? she thought, but to Jerry she said, "How about a definite maybe? Give me a call next week and we'll see, okay?"

There was a pause on the other end. Dawn began to wonder whether the connection had been broken when Jerry heaved a dramatic sigh. "Okay, if that's the best I can get out of you, I guess it'll do . . . for now. But I *will* be calling."

She chuckled. "I'll look forward to hearing from you."

Matt stared out the glass door of his townhouse. He often took his Cessna up on weekends, and today was a good day for flying, the sky cloudless and the winds calm for a change. But last night occupied his mind, not flying. Last night in the Old Oak Corral.

He'd spotted Dawn long before she passed him at the bar. He'd watched her moving gracefully around the dance floor in the arms of the big guy with the black hat. He'd watched as she twirled on the arm of the smaller, blond man, her soft skirt flaring around her legs as they two-stepped briskly over the parquet floor.

Frowning, he remembered her laughing at the table with her admirers gathered around her like a queen holding court. He couldn't recall hearing her laugh before. A light, musical sound, it had brought answering smiles from those on whom she'd bestowed it.

She'd worked with him for two weeks and in that time he'd seen her angry, he'd seen her hurt—he squeezed his eyes shut on that memory—and he'd seen her determined. But he hadn't seen her laughing. The realization made him feel left out, and somehow lonely.

He pulled his hands from his pockets and crossed his arms over his chest as he continued to study, sightlessly, the clear April sky. A prickle of awareness passed over his skin at the remembered feel of Dawn nestled in his arms. She'd been warm, very warm in that crowded room. And she'd smelled so nice. He hadn't wanted to let her go. He sure as heck hadn't wanted to return her to that arrogant cowboy!

He uncrossed his arms and shoved his hands back into his pockets. *What are you doing standing here mooning over her for? She's a career woman, Ivans, and you'd better not forget it.*

Spinning in disgruntlement from the bright vista, he strode to the kitchen bar and snatched up his car keys. The rest of the afternoon he spent at the air strip, vigorously scrubbing and waxing his airplane.

"Good morning, Matt," Dawn greeted pleasantly as she picked up his coffee mug.

He grunted in reply, his attention not wavering from the computer screen in front of him. She raised her eyebrows at his bent head, but said nothing more. When she returned with his fresh cup of coffee, she set it quietly in its place and turned to her own desk, nearly missing his softly muttered, "Thanks".

So, he was going to be a bear today. Nothing unusual in that, she supposed. Maybe he just didn't deal well with Mondays.

Feeling more relaxed than she had in ages, she soon found the morning flown, the clock indicating lunchtime. She, Lisa, and Mary planned to try a new Chinese restaurant. Pausing uncertainly behind Matt, she asked, "I'm going out for lunch today. Could I bring you back something?"

"That'd be great, thanks," he muttered.

"What would you like?"

"Anything."

"Matt, are you all right?"

He threw her a quick glance over his shoulder. "I'm fine," he grumbled. "You know how hectic Mondays are. Just get me a burger and fries, okay?" He tilted forward in his chair to reach for his wallet.

"Don't worry about it; we can settle up when I come back," she assured him, feeling less than sure of herself. Something seemed to be bothering him.

An hour later she set Matt's lunch at his elbow along with the receipt, then hung her suit jacket on the back of her chair while he dug out his wallet.

"I got you the special," she offered pleasantly. "They were featuring a double cheeseburger and large fries today."

"Thanks, that's fine. Here you go."

As Dawn accepted the money, the difference in Matt's behavior crystallized. He'd withdrawn, erected a barrier between them. Nothing overt or aggressive, but rather a quiet folding in on himself. He wouldn't even look her in the eye. She found it very unsettling.

The afternoon wore on, and her earlier sense of ease dissolved. She'd felt so positive when she came to work this morning. She knew her job pretty well by now and was confident that she performed it satisfactorily. She also knew essentially what to expect from Matt Ivans and no longer feared his outbursts. This side of him, however, was something new. It made her uneasy.

He remained quietly polite for the rest of the day, and she tiptoed around him as though he were an invalid.

Tuesday's atmosphere echoed the day previous. Matt continued to be uncommunicative and withdrawn. Not in the best of moods herself, Dawn dampered her morning greeting.

In the middle of the afternoon she stepped up quietly behind Matt to drop a stack of applications in his basket. Unaware of her presence, he swiveled his chair and collided with her, hard. She yelped and jumped back.

"Blast it, Dawn! Do you have to sneak up on me like that?"

"I was just putting these on your desk!"

"Well, the way you've been pussyfooting around, how the heck am I supposed to know you're there?" Then, belatedly he asked, "Are you all right?"

"I'm fine," she grumbled, rubbing her shin. "It's you who needs to be examined."

"I mean," he said with strained patience, "did I hurt you?"

"The damage is minimal. I'll probably have a bruise but that's all."

"Sorry, I didn't know you were there."

"So you've said. Maybe I'll start wearing a bell."

They passed the rest of the day in peevish silence, speaking only when absolutely necessary, last week's camaraderie no longer in evidence.

That evening when Dawn showered, she found to her disgruntlement that she did indeed have a bruised lump on her shin where Matt had kicked her.

Matt soaked in the tub of steaming water, trying to soak the soreness out of his scarred right leg. When he'd swiveled his chair into Dawn, his foot struck her, twisting inward sharply and aggravating the patched network of bone and muscle in his lower limb. Leaning forward, he rubbed it firmly, trying to knead away the discomfort.

In spite of his best home remedies, he had to use his cane the next day. While unselfconscious about his injury, he felt foolish that bumping into that little bit of a woman could incapacitate him. It didn't do his surly disposition a bit of good.

He heard the metallic tinkle when Dawn picked up his coffee cup and a small grin tugged at the corners of his mouth. So the kitten wore a bell, did she? It surprised him that she'd tease about it after they'd both been so snappish yesterday.

When she returned he saw that she wore, not a bell, but a charm bracelet. Still, he wondered if it weren't meant to serve the same purpose. Glancing at her legs, he saw the discolored swelling on her left shin and winced.

"That's some bruise," he offered quietly. "I hope it doesn't feel as bad as it looks."

"Almost." Her words crackled with ice as Dawn nodded to the cane resting beside his desk. "But you really shouldn't have bothered, you didn't quite cripple me."

Matt's eyes widened then his brows dropped into a scowl and a warm flush colored his face. Spinning away to hide his chagrin, he thought it was what he deserved for trying to be nice.

Dawn didn't go out for lunch that day, and didn't offer to bring him anything from the vending machines. He'd be hanged if he'd ask her to, either! Mid-afternoon, his stomach began to growl, so he reached for his cane and levered himself out of his chair.

Dawn noticed the awkward movements out of the corner of her eye, but didn't turn to look at Matt until he'd moved off down the hall. Her jaw dropped open at the sight of him shuffling slowly away, the cane aiding his progress. Her heart fell to her toes before bouncing back up to choke her.

Oh sweet Lord, the cane's for him, not me! Dawn, you idiot!

You complete and total idiot! You've really done it this time!
Her throat closed over unshed tears of humiliation.

The building was practically deserted at 7:30 in the morning, but Dawn had to talk to Matt before the office filled with
curious bystanders. She knew he'd be here. He came early
and stayed late. She'd once wondered fancifully if he didn't
sleep at the bank.

Walking down the hall, she had the depressing thought that
they seemed to be establishing a regular pattern of disastrous
confrontations. She approached his desk and set a Styrofoam
cup of fresh coffee in front of him. "We have to talk."

Matt turned his chair slowly, cast a wary eye at the foam
cup, then looked up at her. "Does this mean you aren't going
to make coffee anymore?"

She quickly suppressed a smile. "No, it only means I
wanted to talk before I made the coffee."

"Okay." He popped the plastic lid off the cup and inhaled
before taking a sip and nodding in approval. "So talk."

"Matt, I'm sorry about what I said yesterday. I . . . I thought
you were being sarcastic and had brought the cane for me. I
had no idea you'd been hurt," she added with a small gesture
that took in his cane as well as his leg. "I don't usually make
such insensitive remarks."

He eyed her skeptically as he took another sip of the steaming coffee. "Are you sure?"

Before she could stop herself, she retorted, "Of course I'm
sure!" Her hands flew to cover her face and she dropped into
her chair, facing him, but hiding from his sight.

He waited in silence. She sighed and lowered her hands to
her lap. "Why does this keep happening?"

"I don't know." A grin creased one side of his face. "It
could be the hair trigger on your temper, I suppose. But besides that, we do seem to have a knack for zeroing in on each
other's sore spots, don't we?"

"I'm afraid so." She nodded toward his foot. "What happened? Did you sprain it?"

"Something like that," he hedged. "Bumping into you just

aggravated an old injury. Don't worry, I'll be fine in a couple of days."

"Well, I am sorry for what I said."

"Forget it." He motioned to her bracelet of jangling Mexican pesos with the cup of coffee. "A new set of bells?"

She didn't quite conquer the smile this time. "Well, I thought it couldn't hurt."

He laughed, then asked seriously, "Why were you slipping around like that, anyway?"

"I don't know. It just seemed that you were troubled by something, so I was trying to stay out of your way, I guess."

Smart lady. Aloud, he said, "Well, next time just ask. I'd rather have you nagging me than sneaking up on me."

"I wasn't sneaking!"

He grinned. "I know."

She'd done it again. The man could set her off without half trying! "You did that on purpose."

"Yup." His eyes were twinkling as he drained the foam cup and tossed it at his wastebasket. "Time to make the coffee."

Their talk relaxed the atmosphere between them again, and Dawn worked with a renewed sense of ease. She felt badly when Matt struggled to his feet sometime later, even though it really wasn't her fault. Leaning heavily on his cane, he returned with the report he'd gone for and behind her Dawn heard his supervisor call to him.

"Matt, the leg's acting up again. What happened?"

Her hands fell still on the keyboard.

"Nothing much, Bill, it'll be okay in a couple of days. I just ran up against an immovable object is all."

Dawn glanced over her shoulder. She couldn't see Matt's face, but she could hear the smirk in his voice.

"Well, you take it easy and stay off the football field," Bill joked, then added, "If you need any time off, just say so."

"Thanks, but I don't think so. It's doing better already."

In a pig's eye! If this was what better looked like, she'd hate to see worse. Matt dropped into his chair with a grunt and propped the cane against his desk. He caught her watching him and cocked a challenging eyebrow in her direction.

"I could have gotten that for you," she offered.

"I suppose you could have, but I needed the walk. It gets worse if I don't try to stretch it once in a while." Then with a smirk he added, "Nice of you to be concerned, though."

Dawn ignored his attempt to bait her, realizing now that it was a game with him. Instead she smiled sweetly. "If you're trying to make me feel guilty, boss man, it won't work. I didn't bump into you, you bumped into me."

"Ah, but I wouldn't have turned just then if I'd known you were hovering right next to me."

"I didn't hover, I approached, and I wouldn't have been so quiet about it if you hadn't been acting like a bear with a sore paw all day," she replied pleasantly.

"Humph," he grunted. Matt didn't know if he was ready for this new stage of their working relationship, one that included verbal thrusts and parries, with her scoring the most points. "If you want grumpy like a bear, I can go back to yelling, you know," he muttered while his inner voice railed, *I wouldn't have been acting like a bear if it hadn't been so nice dancing with you Saturday night. If you didn't smell so good. Feel so good. If you weren't so pretty. If . . .*

Dawn laughed, surprising him. "I've no doubt that you will, the very next time something doesn't suit you. In the meantime, I plan to enjoy the relative calm and get some work done. But if you need me to fetch or carry, just ask."

Matt studied her profile for a few minutes after she turned back to her terminal. Long lashes, delicate nose, softly rounded chin. All in all, a very nice package. Gloomily he turned back to his own desk.

"Lisa, do you know if Matt ever played football in college? Or maybe even professionally?"

"I don't know, why?"

"Well, we sort of ran into each other the other day, literally that is, and he hurt his foot. He said it was an old injury, but he's having to use a cane this week. When Bill asked him about it, he said something to Matt about staying off the football field until it got better."

"Oh, that. No, Matt jokes about it being a 'football knee', is all."

"Oh." Dawn's face drew into a puzzled frown as she continued to set the table.

"You do know what happened, don't you?" Lisa called from the kitchen.

"No, I don't."

"He was injured when his helicopter crashed."

Dawn's hands fell still. "Crashed?"

"Um-hum. Mr. Ivans used to be an Army pilot. His unit was on maneuvers when his helicopter developed engine trouble or something. Anyway, the doctors thought they'd have to amputate the leg, but he wouldn't let them. They put it back together with steel rods and stuff and patched and grafted the muscles. They didn't think he'd ever be able to use it again, but as you've seen, he does very well with it." Lisa grinned. "He can even dance."

Dawn listened with a growing respect for her irascible boss, as well as a growing sense of horror. Her stomach rolled and bile choked her as her churlish remark about not being crippled took on a whole new depth of insensitivity.

Friday afternoon, Dawn received a call from Lisa asking if they were riding home together, or if Jerry would be picking her up from work.

"No," Dawn replied, "I'll ride home with you. I want to change into something more casual, jeans maybe, before we leave."

When she hung up, she found Matt studying her. She flashed him a quick smile and resumed her work.

"Big date tonight, huh?" he asked.

"Hardly, just a burger and a movie."

"Ah. Which of last week's circle lucked out—the big guy in the black hat?"

Dawn chuckled, remembering Jerry's possessive posturing in front of her boss. "Yes, as a matter of fact, it is."

Matt just grunted and let the conversation drop. Well, she seemed darned pleased with herself about it! Who would have thought she'd be snowed by a jerk like that? No accounting for taste.

He sat with his shoulders hunched and his eyebrows curled tightly as he ranted to himself. He didn't hear her until she repeated his name.

"Matt?"

"Hmm?"

"I asked what your plans were for the weekend. Are you going to spend Easter with your family?"

"Oh. Yeah, I'll fly up tomorrow morning and back Sunday evening." Somehow he couldn't inject any enthusiasm into his tone.

"Fly? They aren't nearby?"

He swiveled his chair around to face her and relaxed back in it. "No, all my people are in Colorado. My father has a small spread in a canyon that cuts up into the foothills of the Rockies above Colorado Springs. My next oldest brother works for a computer company there in town, and my oldest brother and his wife have a shop in old Colorado City. They sell trinkets to tourists."

"That sounds profitable. Well, have a nice weekend."

Matt realized as she stood and pushed her chair in that it was quitting time. "You too," he muttered absently, aware of a growing irritation. In a short while she would be setting out for an evening with that hot shot from the Old Oak Corral. He forced his eyes to remain on his monitor, not allowing them to follow her as she walked away, leaving the building, and him, for the weekend.

Chapter Four

While it had been nice to get out and make use of her social skills again, Dawn would not call the evening an unqualified success. The hamburgers were good, delicious in fact, but Jerry chose to take her to the latest "macho man annihilates the bad guys" movie. It had enough martial arts moves and explosive ordinances in it to level Dallas and its population. The only female in the picture appeared trussed on the roof of the building wherein the bad guys had holed up, thus preventing the avenging hero from blowing it off the face of the earth. He would have to use "finesse" to dislodge them. It had been all Dawn could do not to dissolve in hysterical laughter at that line!

When, in the final scene, the woman demonstrated her appreciation to the bloodied and begrimed hero under the illumination of helicopter search lights, Dawn was certain she was going to start laughing . . . or gagging. Jerry, however, chose that moment to squeeze her shoulders and exclaim, "Wasn't that a great movie?" It had taken her several moments to accept that he was serious!

In spite of that, she allowed him a quick goodnight kiss when he left her at her door. She did not, however, commit herself to spending more time with him. He good-naturedly gave up trying to pin her down to another date and left, promising to call later.

Now she sat with the morning paper and a cup of coffee as the small washing machine churned away on her first load of laundry. Lisa came out of her room and padded sleepily to the cupboard for a mug. As she poured herself a cup of invigorating caffeine, the telephone rang.

"If that's Jerry, I'm asleep," Dawn cautioned.

Lisa's eyebrows rose in question, but she reached for the telephone. It was Doug, not Jerry, and Dawn sighed in relief. That ensured the line would be tied up for a couple of hours, at least.

Easter Sunday shone bright and clear, if a little cool at the foot of the Rockies. The whole family had gone to church and then enjoyed the big dinner Matt's mother and sisters-in-law had prepared. Now Matt sat on the porch watching his brothers play ball with their older children.

His oldest brother, Pete, had a son, Pete Junior, age eight, and a daughter, Deanne, six. Pete's youngest, a three-year-old girl named Missy, leaned on the arm of her Uncle Matt's chair holding the stuffed bunny he'd brought her. Luke, the middle brother, had two boys, Mark, almost seven and John, five. Matt's brothers had followed their mother's lead, giving their sons New Testament names.

His hand rose to smooth the curls on Missy's head as he wondered absently if he would ever have any children to contribute to the game. He'd never thought about it before.

"Unc' Matt?"

"What, Missy?"

"You gots a boo-boo on you toe?"

"What?" The toddler stared at his cane. He knew the children had been cautioned not to climb all over him like they usually did.

"Oh, yes, I bumped it, but it'll be okay."

"I bump my knee," the child exclaimed proudly as she pushed the skirts of her frilly Easter dress out of the way to display a rainbow-printed bandage.

"You sure did," Matt praised her as he lifted her to sit on his healthy leg. "Since we both have boo-boos we'll just sit here in this chair and watch the others play a game for us, okay?"

" 'kay. Did you cry?"

Matt chuckled. "No, not this time. Did you?"

"A li'l bit. Mommy made it better."

Matt hugged the little girl and murmured, "Mommies are good at that, aren't they?"

Unexpectedly, a vision of Dawn Miller comforting a weeping toddler flashed through his mind. Why not, he thought, she'd probably be pretty good at it. In spite of her quick flashes of temper, he'd had ample opportunity to observe her nurturing instinct. It showed in the way she'd bring his lunch, in her wearing the jangling bracelets . . . well, that could be self-defense, he supposed . . . in her separating him and the cowboy before either man could start something.

Yes, there were definitely some warm, tender traits buried in that stubborn, efficient career woman. A scowl replaced the tranquil expression that thoughts of her engendered. He wondered about her Friday-night date, and what she might be doing now. An unwelcome picture of her curled up next to the stocky, dark-haired character from the Old Oak Corral replaced his earlier vision. His jaw clenched and he muttered a curse under his breath.

Matt's brothers and their families had gone home, so he walked alone around the yard, easing his stiff leg.

His mother Dee crossed the lawn and joined her youngest son, slipping an arm through his. She smiled up at him mischievously. "Had any strawberry milkshakes lately?"

Matt frowned, but a telltale flush softened the effect. He growled, "Not lately."

"Well, something's bothering you. What is it, son?"

Matt continued to walk slowly, his mother's hand tucked in his arm. They always could talk. She might be able to help him sort things out, assure him he was right.

"I don't know." He sighed. "I thought I had my life all mapped out, you know? I was happy in the Army; I expected to stay there until I retired. Now all I do is push paper all day long, wheeling and dealing for bankers. It's not a bad job, I don't mean that, it just seems I should be doing something more with my life."

"I know, dear. I read somewhere that life is what happens to us while we're making plans for living it."

Matt gave her a dry chuckle.

"I don't suppose you're seeing anyone yet?"

"If by that you mean, do I have a steady girlfriend, no."

"Why not? You've been there long enough to meet people."

"You sure are getting nosy in your old age, aren't you?"

"Mind your manners, Matthew. Mothers are entitled to be nosy; it's in the fine print on your birth certificate."

"I believe it!"

"And you're not going to avoid the question by sidetracking me with your grouching," Dee warned.

He grinned down at her. "Well, it was worth a try."

"You need a new focus for your life, you know, one to replace your military career. You need someone to care about who will care about you. Why aren't you looking for a wife, Matthew?"

"I didn't know I was supposed to be," he grumbled, then softened his tone. "Besides, I didn't think one went 'looking for a wife'. I thought you just invited ladies out whose company you think you might enjoy, until the day you discover one too special to take back home again, so you keep her."

It was Dee's turn to chuckle. "I guess that's pretty much the way it works, but you don't seem to even be enjoying anyone's company."

"No, not often. Maybe it's because I work with so many women all day long. I hear them complaining about their men, fussing at their kids, and making catty remarks about one another. At the end of the day all I want is peace and quiet."

He paused to rub the back of his neck. "Besides, I put in long hours. I'm usually in the office an hour or so early and don't leave until long after everyone else is gone."

"I doubt you'd be at the office so much if you had someone at home you wanted to be with," his mother observed sourly.

"And you're letting the brass section distract you from the flutes."

"What?"

"You know very well what I mean. The woman you're looking for will be sitting quietly somewhere, doing her job, and probably smiling at the petty complaints of her coworkers."

Patting his arm, she continued, "For the most part, the griping and complaining are just one of the ways women relate to one another. Most of it isn't in earnest."

Matt looked at his mother dubiously.

"It's just a way of communicating," she insisted, obviously annoyed with his obtuseness. Suddenly, she changed direction. "Matt, did you fire the girl with the strawberry milkshake?"

"What? No, of course not."

"Why not?"

"In the first place, I wouldn't be able to prove she'd done it intentionally, and in the second place, I would lose the best assistant I've ever had."

"Really? She worked out after all, then?"

Matt avoided looking at her. His eyes fastened, instead, on Pike's Peak, its snow-crested tip crowned in fluffy white clouds. "Yeah, I guess you could say that."

"Tell me."

He hesitated, turning them back toward the house. This would take some time, and he needed to sit down again. "I don't know how to start."

"Start from the day she first came to work for you. It hasn't been that long ago, has it?"

It had been a lifetime ago. Months and months, surely. No. No, only three weeks. Tomorrow would begin their fourth week together.

They climbed the steps to the wide porch, Matt putting his weight on the handrail. He held the screen door for his mother then followed her into the large family room and settled himself in one of the big plaid recliners.

When he finished relating the events of the past three weeks, as honestly as he could, he leaned back with his hands folded behind his head and met his mother's gaze. His father had come in sometime during the recital and pretended to read the paper, but the tilt of his head told Matt that he'd missed nothing.

"So, Mom, you see there can't possibly be anything there. Half the time we get along like cats and dogs. I'll just have to keep looking."

He wondered at the small grin that tugged at the corner of his father's mouth.

"I'd say that depends on what you think you're looking for, wouldn't you?" his mother replied. "If you want a quiet little soul with no opinions of her own, who will look to you to make all the decisions and take care of all the problems, then yes, you need to keep looking.

"But think about it. What kind of mother would a woman like that be? If she's too unsure of herself to state her views when they differ from yours, how can she raise her children to have any self-esteem?" She paused to straighten the doily on the sofa arm beside her, then pinned him with an earnest gaze. "If she needs you to answer all her questions, how are you going to feel when you come home, tired and stressed, only to have to handle all the domestic crises and decisions as well?"

"But isn't that what a man's supposed to do, take care of his family?" Matt challenged.

Walter rustled his paper as he folded it, gaining his wife's attention. Silently they communicated and she nodded to him.

"Son," he began quietly, "for the life of me I can't figure out where you got some of your notions. I guess by the time you came along, things were running so smoothly you never realized how they got done.

"For the years I worked in the mines, who took you and your brothers to the doctor when you broke a bone, or came down sick? Who did the shopping, gave piano lessons, checked your homework, organized school carnivals? The kind of woman you're talking about couldn't do most of that. And that's just a very small part of what a mother does for her children.

"What about what a wife does for her husband?" He tossed a quick smile to his blushing wife and teased, "Besides the obvious, of course. When I'd come in bone tired and sore, I could go soak in a hot tub. I'd get out to a warm meal waiting for me, and you boys all clean and ready for bed to remind me why I went out each morning.

"If your momma needed my input on something, she brought it up after I was clean, fed, rested, and loved. Then we talked it out. If she had a thought on the matter, generally that's the way we went, because she dealt with you kids and the house on a day-to-day basis. I wouldn't have wanted to pick what color the kitchen should be painted. Hell's bells, she's the one who spends the most time in there, not me."

He shifted in his chair, crossing one ankle over the opposite knee. "Sure, an opinionated woman can be a trial sometimes, but you won't get bored with her." Smiling tenderly at his wife he added, "You learn to work things out, and you hope to high Heaven she doesn't get bored with you.

"Another thing, the kind of woman who has to sit and wait for her husband to take care of things is not the kind who can hand him his dream. You know, without your momma, we wouldn't have this place. She's the one who came up with the rest of the money we needed to get it. Money she'd saved from her piano playing. The music lessons, playing for weddings, all that."

The warm look that passed between his parents embarrassed Matt to witness. "No, son, no clinging vine of a woman could do all that. I might be wrong, but I don't believe that's what you really want. I can't see you being happy with that kind of woman."

It was the longest speech Matt could ever remember his father giving, except for the time he'd planned to pick a girl up for the first time in his newly acquired car. Then, like now, Walter had delivered an honest monologue. That time it had been on a man's responsibilities in honoring and protecting the woman he was escorting.

Matt lowered the recliner's footstool and rubbed his leg absently. "But that's just my point, Dad. A career woman is not going to be at home doing all those things. It's a lot different if you have a working wife."

"Matthew, you're an absolute throwback to the Stone Age," his mother scolded. "All wives are 'working wives'. Some choose to devote themselves to homemaking, while others choose to work outside the home as well. And still others have no choice in the matter at all. Yes, if you marry a girl who wants to work outside the house there will be more compromises to make, but it's being done all the time. That's no excuse for not trying to find someone to share your life."

"You think on it, son, and on what your momma tells you. She's a very smart lady."

"Well," Dee exclaimed softly, flushed with pleasure at her husband's praise, "I guess that's probably about all the interfering you're up to for this trip. But you know where to find us when you want to talk. I'm going to pack up some of the leftovers for you to take back with you. I know you aren't eating right."

Matt laughed. Leave it to his mother to lighten the mood. He certainly would think over what his parents said. They had what he wanted. He'd be foolish not to explore their philosophy on what it took to get it, but he still didn't think Dawn Miller fit the bill. Too bad.

"Good morning," Dawn greeted cheerfully, remembering that Matt didn't seem to be a Monday person, but doing it anyway. As expected, he shot her a scowl and merely grunted in reply. She ignored his response, setting about her morning routine in high spirits.

Her humming when she returned with his coffee evidently annoyed Matt. He slammed down his pencil and swiveled his chair to face her. "You certainly are the chirping bluebird of happiness this morning," he challenged. "Is there something you're wanting to tell me?"

She looked up, surprised. "Like what?"

"Like you're engaged to be married and will be leaving our cozy little family in two weeks?"

She started laughing, but when Matt continued to scowl at

her, she struggled to bring it under control. Fighting to keep the smile off her face, she ventured, "You're hung over, right?"

"Of course not!"

"You're on medication and having a bad reaction?"

"What the blazes are you talking about?"

She began to laugh again. "That should be *my* question."

Chagrin written across his face, he dropped his gaze to his lap where his hands were tightly locked together. "I'm just wondering why you're so blasted cheerful this morning, that's all," he grumbled.

"Oh. Well, why don't you simply ask?"

He shot her a malevolent glare.

Undaunted, she smiled in return. "Spring often makes people cheerful. The improved weather, flowers, all that stuff. Personally, I usually get a good dose of optimism following Easter. You know, like there's hope after all?"

"Hope for what?"

"Mankind, life, love, liberty." Dawn tilted her head and studied him a moment before asking, "Why are you so grumpy? Your visit with your family not go well?"

Matt sighed and relaxed back in his chair, turning slightly to reach for the cup she'd brought him. "As a matter of fact, I had a very nice visit, thank you. The weather was clear, the kids well and glad to see me, Mom's cooking is hard to beat, and Dad and I had a good talk."

"Then why are you grumping around?"

He chuckled. "I don't know, habit maybe."

She wrinkled her nose at him. "Is that maybe a habit you could break? It's a definite downer as far as office morale goes."

Matt watched her over the rim of his cup as he took a slow drink. When he lowered the mug he fought the answering smile twitching at the corners of his mouth. "I suppose I could give it a try, if you'll try to control your temper," he teased.

She had the prettiest brown eyes, and right now they were sparkling with mischief.

"Hey, I'll have you know I've made great strides in that

area," she protested in a tone of feigned hurt. "I didn't fly off the handle at you just now, did I?" The mischief touched her smile this time. "I asked very nicely if you had a problem."

Time to end this byplay before he said or did something really stupid, like lean over and kiss her. He saluted her with his upraised cup. "True, you did. Now that the mornings pleasantries are out of the way, what say we get to work?"

He turned back to his desk and Dawn studied his broad back for a moment before getting up the nerve to ask, "What kids?"

"Hmm?"

"You said the kids were well and happy to see you. What kids?"

Laughter evident in his tone, he answered, "My nieces and nephews."

Dawn couldn't say why his reply made her so happy.

Dawn brought him gumbo and cornbread for lunch, but his dark mood from this morning had returned.

"You don't like gumbo?" she asked, mistaking the reason for his mood. "I'm sorry, next time I think about bringing you anything besides a burger, I'll call first."

"I didn't say I disliked it."

"Then what?"

"Nothing. Thanks."

Matt turned back to his desk, effectively dismissing her. Tension tightened the muscles between his shoulder blades as he waited for Dawn to comment on her flowers. Half-a-dozen red roses interspersed with sprigs of baby's breath and couched in lacy fern were arranged in a sparkling cut-glass vase. He wished he hadn't peeked at the card. *Thank you for Friday night. I hope we can do it again, SOON! Jerry.* Now he wondered, with ill humor, just what it was the man wanted to do again, *soon!* The ringing telephone jangled his nerves and interrupted his thoughts.

"StarAmerica Bank, Dawn Miller speaking. Oh, hello, Jerry. I'm fine. Thank you for the flowers. They're beautiful, but I really wish you hadn't done it."

Matt unashamedly eavesdropped.

"I'm sorry, Jerry, I told you I can't this weekend, I'm already committed." She picked up a pencil and began drumming it against the edge of her desk. "Yes, all weekend. We'll see. Maybe in a couple of weeks, okay?" An exasperated sigh. "Jerry I need to get back to work. Thank you again for the roses, they're beautiful. 'Bye."

When Matt glanced back at her over his shoulder, Dawn was gently massaging her temples, eyes closed.

"Friday night not go well?" he inquired, echoing her phrase from the morning.

She gave him a noncommittal grunt.

"Want to talk about it?"

"Thanks, but there's nothing to talk about."

"Are you sure?"

"Yes. Why?"

He shrugged. "Just curious, I guess."

"You need to brush up on your office etiquette for modern men," she scolded. "Curiosity like that could be construed as sexual harassment, you know."

"You're kidding!"

" 'Fraid not."

Shaking his head, he chuckled. "I don't want the salacious details, for Pete's sake, I just wondered whether you'd knocked him on his can."

Dawn leaned back in her chair and laughed. "No, nothing like that. He was the perfect gentleman. It's just that his idea of a good movie turned out to be a mayhem-and-gore action flick where the blood ran ankle-deep."

"Is that all?" He feigned innocent bewilderment on behalf of misunderstood men everywhere. "Now you're not even going to give the guy a second chance?"

"I might, but not soon. Besides, I got the impression the other night that you didn't especially like him."

His good humor fully restored, he laughed. "I don't."

Wednesday afternoon, Dawn was just closing up her desk, ready to leave for the day, when Matt returned from a meeting. She noticed he'd left his cane behind, and barely limped now.

"Looks like you've almost recovered from our run-in."

He glanced down at his leg. "Yeah, I told you it was nothing."

She cocked a challenging brow at him and agreed sarcastically, "Sure, Matt."

"Really, it's no big deal."

"Well, I'm glad you're doing better." She picked up her purse and switched off her terminal. "Another day, another dollar. See you in the morning."

She was a half-dozen paces away from him when he called out. "Dawn?"

She stopped and turned. He was leaning against his desk, arms crossed over his chest. She wished her pulse wouldn't go all funny every time he did something like that.

"Are you really tied up all weekend?" he asked.

"What?"

"You told Jerry you were tied up all weekend. Did you make that up?"

A grin pulled at the corners of her mouth. "Well," she drawled, counting items off on her fingers, "I do need to do my laundry, wash my hair, give myself a manicure, and go to the grocery store. Oh, and do my share of the housework. If spaced properly, those things can take up a whole weekend."

Matt threw back his head and laughed. An appealing movement that really set her heart to racing. When he looked at her again, amusement was still written on his face, along with something else. Uncertainty?

"Would you go out with me this weekend?"

Surprise rendered her speechless for a moment. "What?"

"No blood-and-guts movies, I promise." He raised one hand in pledge, his eyes riveted on hers.

She swallowed. This didn't seem like a good idea.

"Your sister and her friend can come along if it'd make you feel better," he cajoled, "but then Jerry would know you lied to him."

"I . . . I didn't lie."

Matt smiled. "No, that's right, you didn't. How about it? We could have dinner and listen to some music. I know a great little steakhouse out on Highway Twenty. Did you like Ross Tudor? He'll be singing there Saturday night."

Matt's voice was soft and gently persuasive, its effect on her nervous system even more pronounced than his low growl. This definitely was *not* a good idea.

"No funny stuff either," he added.

She drew a deep breath to make her apologies, only to hear herself say, "Thank you, that sounds very nice."

After a stunned pause, she recovered enough to smile and add, "And yes, I like Ross Tudor. That's how Lisa talked me into going with her, too."

"Oh, really?" Matt tilted his head and studied her. "Maybe we should go somewhere else then, where I won't have to compete for your attention if I want to talk to you."

She wrinkled her nose at him. "Good night, Matt. See you in the morning."

Supremely pleased with himself, Matt watched her go. He'd asked and she'd accepted. He only hoped she didn't have a crush on the singer!

Chapter Five

Thankfully, the last two days of the work week passed without incident. Dawn could hold her own when necessary, but she much preferred harmony and routine. Glancing at Matt's back as she stood, she pushed her chair under the desk for the final time today.

He'd been a perfect gentleman ever since she'd accepted his dinner invitation, his attitude strictly business. If only she hadn't found herself more and more attuned to him on a personal level as the time for their date approached. In fact, her awareness of Matt as a man had grown to the point of over-shadowing her perceptions of him as her boss.

The subject of her thoughts chose that moment to stretch his arms over his head, clasping one wrist with the other hand as he straightened his elbows. Then he lowered his arms and rotated his head and shoulders in an obvious attempt to ease his knotted muscles. His neck was thick and corded, but not disproportionately so. He looked up and smiled at her and her heart skipped a beat.

"That time already?" he asked.

"Uh, yeah, I mean yes. Yes, it is," she finished softly, hoping her face didn't look as warm as it felt.

He didn't seem to notice. "Well, I guess I'll see you tomorrow, then. I'll pick you up about seven-thirty, if that's okay?"

"Seven-thirty is fine."

He smiled again and she felt herself grow warm all over. How ridiculous! There sat the same man who had bullied, aggravated, and mercilessly teased her for a month. Just because he'd invited her to dinner was no reason to melt into a puddle.

Regaining her good sense, she took up her purse and started from the office with a determined stride. She'd barely gotten the six paces again when his warm, honeyed voice stopped her.

"Oh, Dawn?"

Steeling herself she turned back and raised a questioning brow. "Yes?"

"Wear that pretty flowered dress again, would you?"

She nodded mutely and fled, doing her best to keep him from realizing her need to escape as shivers of pleasure ran down her spine.

What on earth is wrong with you, Dawn Louise Miller? You're acting like a fifteen-year-old with her first "real" date! Matt may be a little more mature than most of the men you've dated, but you're a grown woman for Pete's sake. She paused in mid-thought as she waited for the elevator. Who was she kidding? She'd been a child when she married, and she'd married a child. Since her divorce, her only date had been last week with Jerry, also little more than a child, with his strutting machismo.

Oh sure, Jerry might be well into his twenties, with his own small construction company, but maturity was more than the accumulation of years. Maturity came from experiencing what life meted out and surviving it, more or less intact.

Like her, Matt had survived that type of experience. The type that tempers one's character in the fires of pain, that sears one's soul with the memory of loss. No, she was no longer a child. She was, however, unsure of the woman she'd become.

Dawn's hand shook as she tried to fasten her hair back with a small swirled comb. She closed her eyes, counted to five, and concentrated on taking deep, even breaths. Then she brushed back the other side of her thick fall of hair and held it with a matching comb. The mass hung in soft, thick waves just past her collar. Eyeing her reflection critically, she wondered whether the hairdo looked too girlish. She frowned and put on her earrings to see if that made a difference. The white plastic ovals complimented her slender neck nicely, but she still wasn't sure about her hair.

"Oh, Dawn, you look great, I love your hair that way." Lisa's voice was sincere. "It's such a change from the way you wear it to work. Ivans may not recognize you," she teased.

"Not the corporate look, huh?"

"Not at all. You're not by any chance setting out to hook him, are you?" Lisa teased with a grin. Suddenly her expression changed to one of horror. "Oh, Dawn! You're not, are you? You don't need that kind of grief. Honest! Why don't you stick to Jerry? He's nice and safe. You could have him jumping through hoops in no time," Lisa babbled.

Dawn watched her sister's emotional parade with amusement.

A thoughtful frown puckered Lisa's brow as she continued, almost to herself, "However, if you throw Ivans back once he's caught, that would be all right. It might just teach him a lesson."

Dawn laughed. "Lisa, calm down. I'm simply having dinner with the man, okay? You're the one who's been harping at me to get a life, now you're acting like an hysterical maiden aunt."

Lisa slumped down on the foot of Dawn's bed. "Yeah, I guess I am. If it were anyone but Mr. Ivans, I wouldn't give it a second thought." She sighed, then eyed Dawn critically. "Which reminds me, when we saw him at the Corral, weren't you wearing that same dress? You could wear your peasant skirt and ruffled blouse, or how about your blue dress?"

Dawn turned back to the mirror and began putting on her lipstick. Concentrating on her task, she answered without thought, "No, this dress is fine, it's what Matt wanted me to wear."

She missed the shocked look that dropped her sister's jaw.

They drove into the sunset, the windows open to the sweet spring air. Matt reached over and took her hand, covering it with his on the console between them. She gave him a quick, timid smile then looked out the windshield again to where the sky glowed in shades of pink darkening to purple.

"Pretty, isn't it?" Matt's voice was low and soft..

"Um-hmm."

"You are, too. I meant to tell you that before we left, but your sister didn't let me get a word in edgewise."

Pleasure warmed her, but she forced a small laugh and ignored his compliment in favor of the latter part of his statement. "Yes, Lisa can be quite a talker."

"That she can." He squeezed her hand. "I like your hair that way."

"Thank you." *This is a mistake! How am I ever going to make it through the evening when I get all shaky with every word he says? How will I ever be able to look him in the face again at work? I'll have to quit my job, that's all there is to it. I can move back to Houston, or go to work at the grocery store until I find something else. Or I could—*

"Dawn?"

"Yes?"

"Am I making you uncomfortable? You're awfully quiet."

"Oh, no, not at all. I . . . I was just enjoying the sunset and fresh air."

"You're sure?"

She swallowed. "I'm sure."

"Good."

I'm sure I'm not ready for this, that's what I'm sure of! But what was the big deal? *It's not like this is the first man to touch you since Dave.* No, that had happened the night she went to the Corral and danced with him and with Lisa's friends. *Why is it your single dance with Matt Ivans came to mind before any of the others?*

Matt pulled the bright-blue classic Pontiac Firebird up in front of an adobe-style building. The small marquee on top announced Ross Tudor's performance. He walked around and opened her door, offering his hand as she stepped out, then ushered her through the restaurant door with a touch of his fingertips on the small of her back. The brief contact had her flushing again, making her glad for the room's dim lighting.

Although the building was plain and unadorned, the tables inside were covered in white linen and set with simply patterned china and silver. The crystal was a simple design as well, but crystal nonetheless. Red linen napkins folded into fans sat upright at each place, and red candles burned in small hurricane lamps in the center of each table.

At the front of the room, a small dance floor edged against the curtained stage. Instrumental renditions of country ballads played softly through speakers as Matt gave the hostess his name and they were shown to a secluded table for two, one that had a good view of the stage without being too close.

"This is nice," Dawn murmured.

"I'm glad you like it. The food here is pretty good," he added as he perused his menu.

"Always a sound practice in the restaurant business," she quipped.

Matt cocked an eyebrow at her. "Yes, I guess it is."

Small talk. Neither of them was doing very well at it. Thankfully the waitress arrived and they gave her their dinner orders. Matt was about to speak again when a man seated at the far end of the bar caught his attention. He groaned softly and nodded in acknowledgement of the other man's drink raised in salute.

Dawn glanced toward the bar. "What's the matter?"

"Nothing. Would you like to be introduced to Ross Tudor?"

"Thanks, but I'm not a backstage groupie, Matt."

"Well, he's coming over here."

She turned to look fully in the direction of Matt's gaze. Sure enough, the handsome young singer approached their table with quick strides. Flashing a dazzling, and strangely familiar, grin at her, he held out his hand to her escort.

"Matt, I thought that was you. I'm glad you came out. How's the family?" During his entire greeting, his eyes were on her, not Matt.

"They're fine, Ross," Matt responded flatly. "Dawn, I'd like you to meet my cousin, Ross Tudor. Ross, this is Dawn Miller."

"The pleasure is all mine, pretty lady." Ross's voice oozed like molasses, dark and slow. He turned on that smile again and she recognized it as the same one she'd glimpsed on Matt a time or two recently.

"Cousin?"

"Ross's mother and mine are sisters." Matt didn't sound too happy about their kinship at the moment.

"How nice," she replied politely.

Matt only grunted as Ross stood there grinning like a pirate with a new-found treasure chest.

"Aren't you going to invite me to join you, Cuz?"

"Don't you have to practice or something?"

Ross promptly pulled up a chair and placed it next to Dawn, angling it her way. "Nope, I've already warmed up. My last gig was only in Dallas, so I got here early." He turned dark eyes on Dawn. "Speaking of warming up, how about a dance before your food comes? It'll sharpen your appetite."

Without waiting for her answer, Ross pulled Dawn to her feet. Her eyes sought Matt's in silent appeal, but he was looking at his hands clenched on the table before him. With grave misgivings, she resigned herself to dancing with Ross. Somehow, she didn't think she was going to enjoy this.

"Why so uptight, Sugar? Relax and let ol' Ross take control."

The words, whispered gruffly in her ear, made Dawn shudder with distaste as she found herself pulled into a tight embrace. Ross wasn't as tall as Matt, or as wide, but he was strong enough. Her feeble attempts to put some space between them got her nowhere.

Ross pulled his head back just enough for her to see his grin as he chided softly, "Un-unh, sweet thing, you're not going anywhere. Ol' cousin Matt may be your baby-sitter for the evening, but I sure plan to get to know you better when my show is done. You just settle your head on my shoulder and let me hold you a while, okay?"

It wasn't okay. *Is this why Matt asked me out, to provide a companion for his cousin?* Her mind rebelled. *Those cretins! Those cave-dwelling barbarians! Those filthy simians! Those . . . those . . .* Her pointed heel came down with force on Ross's instep.

"Oww! What in thunder did you do that for?"

"Sorry, guess I'm not very good at dancing cheek to cheek," she bit out, with far more challenge in her voice than remorse. "You'll just have to find another partner."

Ross studied her for a minute, then took another step back from her and made a slight bow. "The apology should be mine, ma'am. No offense intended." He gestured to her table, and followed behind her at a safe distance.

"Thank you for the dance, Miss Miller. Good seeing you, Matt."

Dawn refused to look at either of the men. In fact, she was contemplating picking up her purse and calling a taxi, when she became aware of Ross pulling out her chair to seat her. She slid into the waiting chair, her cheeks still burning with outrage, her mind racing for an escape from this humiliating situation. She should never have come.

Ross moved away from Dawn and gently thumped his older cousin on the shoulder, before offering softly, "Congratulations, Cuz, looks like you've got a keeper there."

Dawn sat in silence, her gaze directed out the window beside her, the edge of her lower lip caught between her teeth.

"Dawn, are you okay?"

She didn't turn at Matt's soft inquiry, but nodded in reply.

"He isn't a bad kid, he just lets his reviews go to his head sometimes. I'm sorry."

She raised her chin a notch and skewered him with outrage flashing from the depths of her topaz eyes.

"Are you?" she asked coldly. At his look of confusion she clarified, "Are you sorry?"

He shook his head imperceptibly, as if to clear it. "Of course I am."

"Why?"

"What do you mean, why?"

"Why are you sorry? Are you sorry because your cousin behaved like a jerk, or are you sorry because I turned him down?"

Matt straightened in his chair, his posture stiff. "I presumed he was a jerk from your reaction, and for that I'm sorry. But what did he say, Dawn? What has you so upset?"

She studied his clenched jaw for a moment, then wilted back against her chair. Of course he wouldn't set her up, he wasn't that kind of man. He wouldn't hesitate to go after what he wanted for himself, but Matt Ivans pandered for no one.

"Forget it," she muttered and reached for her wineglass.

Matt's hand shot out and caught her fingers before they could curl around the stem. He grasped her hand gently, willing her to look at him.

"What did he say?" His voice, though soft, held the unmistakable note of command.

She looked at their joined hands, his so much bigger, so much stronger than her own. Her teeth worried her bottom lip a moment, then she sighed and raised her eyes to his.

"Ross gave the impression that I was to be his companion this evening."

"What?" Matt half rose from his chair, his hands braced on the tabletop, a killing fury in his eyes. "That little son of a . . . I'll break his ever-loving neck!"

"Matt, please, don't make a scene." Dawn grabbed one of his wrists, knowing that should he chose to storm after his cousin, she had no real chance of restraining him. "Please," she implored softly, letting her eyes make their own appeal to the man poised above her.

Slowly Matt sank back into his chair, his gaze never wavering from hers. In a slow, deliberate motion he reached for his drink, took a long swallow from the sweat-slicked glass, then, with the same precise movements, set it back on the table. He watched in stony silence as a drop of moisture made a track on its way down the side of the glass, the muscles in his jaw working.

A sound, more like a bark than a laugh for its lack of mirth, startled Dawn. Matt shook his head. "We sure are a pair, aren't we? We can't seem to find a smooth road no matter what we do."

He seemed so vulnerable in that moment, the expression on his craggy features mirroring the dejection in his voice. She reached for his hand and he turned it palm up, gripping her fingers tightly.

"I'm sorry," he whispered again. "Do you want to go?"

"No," she answered, amazed herself that she really didn't.

"You're sure?"

"And miss my shrimp dinner? I should say not!"

A smile softened Matt's features, but didn't quite light his eyes. "A woman after my own heart. Food first, everything else is secondary."

As if on cue, the waitress arrived with their dinners, a platter of delicately fried butterfly shrimp for Dawn and a lobster tail/ steak combo for Matt. They ate in silence, the tension slipping away in the benign quiet.

Matt wiped his mouth with his napkin, and heaved a sigh of contentment. Dawn smiled in agreement. The food was quite good.

"What would you like for dessert?"

"Not a thing, thanks. Just coffee."

"They have a great cheesecake here, or one of those chocolate concoctions that put you in sugar shock."

"No thanks, just coffee."

Matt leaned his elbows on the table and jutted his head forward as he challenged, "You have no adventure in your soul, Miller."

"I accepted a date with you, didn't I?" she shot back.

He directed his laughter at the ceiling. Dawn watched with interest as amusement transformed his stern features. He really was so good-looking when not looming over a person, scowling.

"Yeah, you did, didn't you," he agreed on a waning chuckle. Their gazes met and held for a moment. A warm smile softened his lips, this one reaching his eyes. "Do you feel adventurous enough to dance with me, or did your experience with Ross traumatize you?"

"I don't traumatize that easily."

His smile became a grin as Matt stood and pulled back her chair. "I didn't think so."

"Then why did you say it?"

He shrugged and pulled her into his arms. "To give you an out, I guess."

They moved smoothly around the floor in silence for several minutes before she spoke again. "Communicating can really be complicated, can't it?"

Matt tilted his head to one side and looked at her. "Would you like for it to be simpler?"

"I don't know. I think so."

"Okay, we can try it for a while and see what happens."

She frowned slightly, started to speak, but changed her mind and lay her head against his shoulder again. *See, already you're avoiding it. You can't handle straightforward communication any more than he can.*

The song ended and a fast number followed, so they returned to their table. Matt signaled the waitress and ordered coffee and cheesecake for two.

"Listening is evidently complicated for some people, too," Dawn observed, her tone censuring.

Matt grinned at her. "If you really don't want it, you don't have to eat it. You women claim to be watching calories when you don't need to be."

She glared at him while she battled with herself. He was the one who suggested they try plain speaking, so why not?

"Matt, I don't like generalizations, and what you just said is one of the worst I've heard in a long time. Don't treat me that way."

He blinked in surprise then cleared his throat. "I did suggest we simplify, didn't I?"

She fought a smile. "Yes, you did."

"Are the terms 'simple' and 'brutal' interchangeable?"

"I wasn't brutal, just honest."

"Brutally honest."

It wouldn't work. She sighed. Direct talk did not take into

account people's feelings, most of which were unreasonably tender, her own included.

"Hey." He reached across the table and took her hand, shaking it gently as he had before. "I'm just kidding. You don't really believe I'm that sensitive, do you?"

"That's just the problem," she answered in exasperation. "I don't believe you're the least bit sensitive, otherwise you wouldn't say such unbelievably stupid things."

"You know, I think you're right." He rested his elbows on the table and leaned his chin on his fists. "It'll take some getting used to. Maybe you could be my sensitivity trainer."

"No thanks."

"Why not? You're not afraid to tell it like it is."

"I don't like stirring up trouble."

Matt laughed again, this time longer than before, and Dawn was frowning by the time he recovered enough to get out, "Yeah, right."

She opened her mouth to speak, but the restaurant owner's introduction of Ross cut off her sharp retort. The curtains parted and Ross acknowledged the patrons' applause with several showy bows. Matt took advantage of the distraction to pick up his chair and carry it around to Dawn's side of their small table. Settling himself beside her he met her startled look with a grin, placed his arm along her chair back, then leaned over and whispered, "Just a message to Ross that you're off-limits, in case he didn't get it earlier."

Dawn nodded and Matt felt absolutely no compunction at misleading her. If it got him close enough to touch her, then it was fair as far as he was concerned. Besides, who knew? Maybe Ross had gotten thick-headed in the last hour. He'd certainly have to be to misread Dawn's rejection.

"Good evening, folks, I hope you're enjoying yourselves. I'm proud to have this chance to entertain you." Ross's spiel was interrupted by more applause. "I'd like to dedicate this first song to my favorite cousin and the special lady he has with him here tonight. Hit it, boys."

People glanced furtively around, trying to discover the identity of the couple mentioned, but neither Ross nor Matt gave anything away.

Matt tightened his arm around her shoulders in a gentle hug as Ross began singing a love song and Dawn wished for a hole to disappear into, wondering why being around him increasingly generated thoughts of escape. *I don't need this, that's why,* she thought. *I don't want some man directing my life.*

Even though his touch makes you feel special?

Even though.

Oh for Heaven's sake, it's just dinner, he isn't asking you to marry him! He hasn't even put a move on you.

Not yet.

Would it be so bad if he did?

I guess not, as long as he takes no for an answer.

Why no?

You know very well why. No commitments, no complications. Never again. I take care of myself.

With Ross's next song, couples filed onto the dance floor.

"Care to dance?" Matt invited.

She nodded. Maybe moving around would help order her jumbled thoughts. Matt took her in his arms, pulling her close. She snuggled her head in the hollow by his shoulder, her cheek against his chest. *Foolish girl, now you can't think at all.*

Dawn sighed. That was okay, too. It would be nice not to have to think about anything for a while. She drifted to the music, warm and secure in a pair of strong arms.

Matt stopped moving and people applauded. Lulled by the comfort of his embrace, Dawn belatedly realized the number had ended. Ross launched into a string of lively, foot-stomping tunes as Matt led her back to their table where coffee and cheesecake waited.

She expected him to put his chair back where it belonged, but he just excused himself as he reached past her to get his dessert. Bracing one ankle on his opposite knee, Matt gave every appearance of a man thoroughly enjoying himself.

"Try a bite," he teased, extending his fork toward her, a large morsel of the rich creation balanced on the tines.

"Matt," she scolded.

"Come on, live a little. No guts, no glory," he coaxed.

"Fat is not glorious."

Dawn could have bitten her tongue. Not only had she given credence to Matt's earlier sexist remark, she'd given him leave to leisurely examine her, sending blood once again flooding to her face.

She endured his inspection in stoic silence. Maybe he wouldn't say anything. Yeah, and maybe it would snow in Fort Worth next July.

"Dawn," his voice flowed like warm honey, "if what I see is fat, then glorious doesn't begin to describe it."

"Cut it out, Matt," she warned through gritted teeth.

Quickly he reverted to teasing her. "I will if you take a bite."

"Oh, all right." She reached for the plate he held, but he pulled it back. Confused, she looked up and encountered a warmth in his eyes that turned them to molten pewter.

"Let me," he whispered as he offered her a taste of the dessert from his fork. Slowly, her gaze held by his, Dawn opened her lips to accept what he offered, feeling as she did so, that she'd accepted more from him than a simple bite of food.

Matt felt it too. She saw the heat kindle in his eyes. Suddenly he dropped his gaze. "That wasn't so bad, was it? Now eat your dessert." His words were light-hearted, but his voice held a strident undertone.

Obediently, she picked up the other plate and ate the entire slice of cheesecake without tasting a single bite. Hands shaking, she lifted her coffee cup and burned her tongue on the hot liquid.

Ross began another slow song and Matt stood, wordlessly pulling her to her feet. Once she was in his arms, he kissed the hand he held, then tucked it between them. His other arm clamped her gently against him and he dropped his cheek to rest it against her forehead. Her senses kicked into overdrive.

Her heart fluttered wildly in her chest and her blood tingled as though fed from an effervescent spring. What was going on here? She'd just been alone too long, that's what.

Dawn drew a shaky breath, hoping he wouldn't notice. She couldn't possibly be reacting to her belligerent boss this way. Not Matt. Not Ivans the Terrible! No way!

Oh, no? It's been happening since the day you first laid eyes on him.

Chapter Six

They left as soon as Ross's show finished. Both quiet, both aware of a subtle change in the atmosphere between them. Neither knew what would come next, neither certain what he *wanted* to come next.

Matt parked in front of Dawn's building and turned off the engine. She waited for him to open her door, but instead of getting out of the car, he turned and draped his arm across the seat behind her shoulders.

"Dawn," he began, but his voice cracked. He cleared his throat and tried again. "Dawn, thank you for having dinner with me. I've really enjoyed this evening."

"Me, too. Thank you for asking me." This felt so stiff, so formal.

"Maybe we could do it again sometime?"

She dropped her gaze. In spite of her better judgment, the words slipped out. "I'd like that."

"Good."

Without looking up, she knew he watched her. They sat in silence a moment, then he slowly reached out his left hand and with a gentle pressure, tipped up her chin. He leaned closer, the arm behind her slid around her shoulders pulling her to him.

She knew Matt was going to kiss her, but she couldn't decide what to do about it. In the end, she did nothing except watch those silvered eyes move closer in the dim light. Her own eyes closed and her world of sight gave way to a world of touch, of taste.

The lips that pressed hers were warm, soft, gentle. Their taste sweet and moist. She sighed her contentment with the tender contact as she reached a hand to the side of his face. Just one kiss. What was the harm? It had been so long, so terribly long.

The kiss, begun as a sweet parting gesture, quickly changed. A desire to erase the loneliness and the pain from their hearts, to find warmth and comfort with another human being . . . a desire to find someone to trust, burned in the kiss now exchanged.

Dawn's heart swelled to fill her chest, the pressure robbing her of breath. Mercy, how she'd missed this, needed this . . . but they had to stop. And they had to stop now.

"Matt." She tried to pull away from him. "Matt," she repeated, louder. "Matt, stop."

He looked at her, his expression confused for a moment, eyes glazed, then he nodded. Drawing in a deep breath, he slowly straightened himself in the seat. He still embraced her with one arm, and as he sat up he tilted her against him across the console, resting his chin on top of her head.

He expelled his breath in one long slow draft, and softly agreed, "You're right, that wasn't a very good idea." In a voice filled with wonder he added, "But I can't remember a kiss I've ever wanted as much."

Dawn looked at her bedside clock. Three A.M. She'd been staring at the ceiling of her darkened room for almost two hours, trying to decide what to do next.

How could she just go into work on Monday and pretend that nothing had changed? That Matt hadn't taken her out, hadn't kissed her senseless, hadn't stirred a hunger she'd thought long dead? She couldn't possibly pull that off.

If she couldn't act as though nothing had happened, she'd have to move on. To another job, another place. She simply would not open herself up to that kind of pain again. She could *not* allow yet another man control of her happiness and well-being. These things were hers to attend to, and she'd never be so defenseless again.

3:30 and Matt hadn't closed his eyes. How could he be so stupid? He knew before he'd touched her that he was asking for trouble.

But she smelled so sweet, like the flowers that climbed the porch trellis back home. And soft. Had he ever touched another woman with skin as soft? Or held one who'd fit against him so perfectly? When she looked at him her eyes held such a wealth of promises. Ah, yes, her eyes.

Dawn was so complex. Matt knew for certain she had no idea that even while she fumed and challenged, her eyes sought approval, acceptance. Yes, she could look daggers of ice from those beautiful brown depths, but most of the time her eyes held just a touch of bewilderment.

That open confusion is what prompted him to kiss her. He'd felt the need to reassure her. Of what, he'd no idea. But the whole thing had turned into a disaster, that much he did know.

A simple good-night kiss, to let her know he enjoyed their evening, to let her know everything was all right, that's what he intended. What he gave her was something altogether different.

He threw an arm over his eyes and groaned aloud. No mistake, he'd given her his entire being, and what he got in return was a branding of his very soul. She'd marked him . . . and the woman didn't even know it.

He cursed and wearily scrubbed his hands over his face. How in the name of Heaven had it happened? She was just a little bit of a thing, barely reaching his shoulder. But his palms remembered the feel of her skin, the contours of her frame, and his hands clenched into fists as he realized she suited him fine. She fit perfectly, just like she was.

Ross might be right, maybe she was his "keeper". Tonight had given him a taste of what he could have with this woman, but what to do about it?

Brooding, Dawn thought she must not have made as much of an impression on Matt as he had on her. He hadn't called yesterday. She covered a yawn and hoped she hadn't made a fool of herself.

Unfortunately, *someone* had called this morning, around 2:00. The man's whispered, "Hiya, babe," had caught her off-guard. When she didn't respond, the raspy-voiced whisper had chided, "Where were you last night? I called early but no one answered." She'd hung up without replying and the phone had rung again immediately. She'd lifted the receiver then replaced it, waiting a moment before unplugging the telephone for the remainder of the night. Whoever the prankster had been, she knew he'd give up sooner or later. Right now her biggest problem was facing her boss.

Squaring her shoulders, she marched down the hall to their cubicle with a brisk, businesslike air. She could do this. She could pretend Saturday never happened.

Her heart ricocheted off her ribs at the sight of Matt bent over his desk, a lock of dark hair falling over his forehead. She quickly averted her gaze.

If she didn't look at him, maybe she could bluff her way through this day. "Hello," she greeted crisply and left with his cup before he could answer.

"Good morning," he replied when she returned with his coffee.

Monday always meant a heavy workload, and today Dawn was glad of it. She and Matt worked without non-essential conversation until lunchtime.

"What do you want for lunch?" she asked as she slung the strap of her purse over her shoulder.

"Nothing today, thanks," he replied with a quick glance at her. He had a client on the telephone so she nodded and left.

Matt's chair was empty when she returned. Maybe he had a lunch date. With a stab of jealousy, she wondered who it could be.

She was on the telephone verifying an applicant's insurance when Matt returned and set something on the corner of her desk. Her back to him, she'd sensed his presence when he stepped near, then retreated. Making the appropriate notes on the form before her, she hung up the phone and turned.

On the corner of her desk sat a pot of pink tulips. She glanced at Matt's back and hesitantly reached for the card. She read: *Simply put, thank you for a wonderful evening. Matt.*

"Thank you, Matt, but this wasn't necessary."

He turned his chair to face her. "Does that mean I don't get another chance, either?" His lips lifted in a teasing smile, but his expression was watchful.

Dawn bit her lower lip as a light blush climbed her cheeks. "I didn't mean that."

"Good."

She reached a finger out and gently touched one of the sturdy blooms. "I'm not sure I know how to care for tulips."

"The instructions are on a card at the back of the pot. Do you know why I chose tulips instead of roses?"

She shook her head slowly, still trying her best not to look at him, but it would be rude not to do so now, so she raised her eyes.

"Because they remind me of spring. You know, renewed hope for mankind and all that?"

Dawn smiled and stroked a flower with the back of her finger. "They're beautiful, thank you."

"You're welcome." Matt studied her a minute more, then his phone rang and he turned to his desk.

Fool! You blew a perfect chance to end it. All you had to do was add "but it wouldn't be a good idea" to your "I didn't mean that". Now the man probably thinks you're hot for him.

Well, if he does, he's not far from wrong, Dawn's conscience argued. She forced her attention back to her job. Maybe tomorrow would be easier.

Of course, Lisa knew about the flowers by the time Dawn met her in the parking lot yesterday afternoon. That didn't bother Dawn, she'd have told Lisa about them herself, but it meant that word had spread through the building that Matt Ivans had brought her flowers. Pulling open the big glass door, she squared her shoulders, raised her chin a notch, and forged ahead.

Embarrassingly, she found herself the recipient of thumbs-up signals, eyebrows arched in disapproval, and eager grins of curiosity from the other women as she made her way to her floor and her work station.

Through most of the morning, she managed to keep her mind on business, thinking of Matt only when she saw him, heard him, or smelled his aftershave. In other words, constantly. Her productivity fell way off. Dawn sighed and rubbed the back of her neck. Maybe she could pull herself together during lunch.

Leaving the bank building, she stepped into the warm spring day and inhaled deeply. This is what she needed, fresh air and sunshine, the required ingredients for putting things into their proper perspective. She had her health, a roof over her head, food to eat, a decent job; what more could she need? *Love?* Dawn pushed that gnawing thought aside and stepped off the curb.

"Dawn, wait up." Matt caught her arm. "Mind if I join you?"

Inwardly she groaned. Of course she minded, but she couldn't very well say so. "No, but I thought I'd get some Mexican food."

"Fine with me," he answered cheerfully. "I know a great little place not too far from here. Everything is homemade."

He ushered her to his car and drove them to the little neighborhood restaurant. The waitress remembered Dawn, and gave Matt a most unfriendly look while solicitously taking Dawn's order. When she returned with their meals, she dropped Matt's plate of enchiladas in front of him with a thump, muttering something about *hombres* under her breath. He watched her departure, puzzled, while Dawn fought to keep from laughing.

"Sorry, the service isn't what it used to be."

Keeping a straight face, Dawn replied innocently, "Oh? I find it to be excellent, as always."

Matt's narrowed eyes bored into her. "You've eaten here before, then?"

Again, the cherubic look of innocence. "Yes, a time or two."

The sturdy dark-haired woman returned to give Dawn an extra bowl of salsa for her chimichangas. "You need anythin' else, Señorita?"

"No, Maria, this is fine, thank you. Matt, do you need anything?" she asked solicitously, enjoying herself after all.

Eying both women with suspicion, he muttered, "No, I'm fine, thanks."

Maria gave him the evil eye again and flounced off. Dawn quickly covered a giggle with her hand and avoided meeting his gaze.

"What the heck is going on here?" he growled softly.

"What do you mean?"

"Don't give me that Miss Innocent look. You know darn well what I mean."

"Mr. Ivans, I've no idea what you're talking about. Don't you like your lunch? Is something wrong with your enchiladas?"

"No, the food is fine, Dawn," he replied through gritted teeth, "but something is definitely wrong with Maria, and I think you're in on it."

"Don't be silly. Now eat your lunch or we'll be late."

She sounded ridiculously like a mother chiding a youngster, but Matt did as she suggested, realizing he wasn't going to get an answer out of her.

"I hear Mr. Ivans took you to lunch today."

Dawn took her eyes from the evening traffic just long enough to glance at her sister. "Sort of. We left for lunch at the same time, so we ate together."

"Sounds like hedging to me. Did he pay for your meal?"

"Yes."

"Then I'd say he took you to lunch, no 'sort of' about it. Dinner on Saturday, flowers yesterday, lunch today . . ." Lisa trailed off speculatively.

"Lisa . . ."

"Dawn, it's your business. Just be careful, okay?"

Dawn drove in silence for several miles, trying to put her thoughts in order before speaking.

"Lisa, there's really nothing to be careful about. I went out with Matt once. I may even do it again sometime, but I don't intend to become involved with him."

"We all know what happens to most good intentions," Lisa muttered glumly.

"I mean it, Lisa. Not Matt or any other man, for that matter."

Lisa bit her lip to keep from commenting.

Wednesday was better for Dawn. She could almost look Matt in the eye again. At lunchtime she slipped out while he was in his supervisor's office. She brought him back a burger and a drink in case he'd stayed in. When she set it on his desk he looked up at her and smiled.

"Just like old times, huh?"

"Just like old times," she agreed. If only her heart would stop going crazy every time he smiled, things could truly get back to normal.

"Too bad," he teased softly, "I was looking forward to the change in routine."

Dawn snatched the money he held out to her for his lunch then spun to her desk as a wave of warmth shimmied up her spine and climbed her neck to her face. Behind her, Matt chuckled.

She left with the other women at the end of the day to avoid being alone with him. She knew she had to get a grip on herself, but every time she thought she'd recovered, he'd laugh or touch her shoulder or do one of a dozen other things that sent her blood racing. He'd only kissed her the one time and she'd become a basket case. She couldn't understand it. Jerry had kissed her too, but that caused her no problem at all.

Back at the apartment, Dawn slipped out of her skirt and hung her suit in the closet. In the next room, the telephone rang. Lisa answered it then called out, "Dawn, telephone."

A clutching sensation gripped Dawn's chest. She stuck her head out of the bedroom and mouthed *"Who is it?"*

Lisa just raised an eyebrow and waggled the receiver in the air. Dawn scowled in return and stomped into the living room in her slip to snatch the offending mechanism from Lisa's hand.

"Yes?"

"Rough day at the office, I take it?" Matt's voice teased.

"As a matter of fact—"

"I understand completely," he interrupted in his soft, honeyed tone, "and I have just what the doctor ordered. How about taking a ride with me Saturday? We could fly over to Austin, have lunch, make like tourists, and be back in time for you to get your beauty sleep."

"That's a lot of driving to do in one day," Dawn answered suspiciously. He would get her there then no doubt plead fatigue and suggest they spend the night.

"I meant it literally when I said we'd fly, Dawn. You know, as in airplane?"

"Airplane?"

Matt's warm laugh filled her ear, working it's magic, lacing her blood with effervescent bubbles. "Yes, airplane. I have a four-passenger Cessna. Maybe Lisa would like to come along?"

It was a testament to the man's power to completely scramble her mind that she actually turned to her sister and asked, "Do you and Doug want to fly to Austin with Matt on Saturday?"

"You've got to be kidding!" Lisa answered, aghast. "Dawn, you know I'm terrified of flying."

"Oh, that's right," Dawn murmured. "No, I'm sorry, Lisa doesn't like to fly," she told Matt.

"Too bad. Okay, I'll pick you up about eight-thirty Saturday morning. See you tomorrow."

The dial tone snapped her out of her trance. "Matt, wait. Matt? Confound him, he hung up," Dawn muttered as she slammed the receiver back into its cradle.

"Why are you going to Austin?" Lisa asked, barely disguising her amusement.

"Austin? I don't know . . . I'm not going to Austin!"

Lisa broke out laughing as the perplexed look on her sister's face changed into a horrible frown. She wasn't comfortable with the thought of Dawn dating Matt Ivans, but the effect the man had on her older sister was comical.

"I think you are," Lisa goaded before breaking into a new round of laughter.

Dawn stalked back to her room and slammed the door, then threw herself onto her bed. She'd lost her mind, there was no other explanation. Well, Matt Ivans would have to go to Austin without her. She'd simply tell him so at work tomorrow. Not only did she have things to take care of on the weekends, she didn't intend to be alone with the man ever again.

Why? a little voice asked, but Dawn didn't want to examine the answer.

"Matt, I can't go to Austin with you Saturday."

Matt raised his eyes to the woman standing beside his desk, clutching his coffee mug in her hands as though it were a shield. "Good morning to you, too," he responded pleasantly.

"Matt," she snapped, clearly exasperated.

He folded his hands behind his head and tipped the chair back, smiling into her flashing eyes. "What's the big deal? You can't work seven days a week, I've tried it. You soon lose your edge, not to mention your mind. Not only is it permissible to relax on weekends, it's essential to a person's mental and physical well-being."

Dawn glared down at him, wishing his smile weren't so appealing. "Somehow I don't think your well-being depends on my flying off to Austin with you."

"Maybe not, but it would be a nice break for both of us. How about it? Just an outing with a friend, okay? No fresh stuff, I promise."

"You promise?" She looked up at him, her head cocked warily to one side.

"I promise. Although it has always been my personal opinion that the automatic pilot was developed for that very reason."

"Matt!"

He raised his palms in surrender. "Okay, okay. I promise."

Dawn had spent two hours Friday evening deciding what to wear for her trip to Austin, but that didn't keep her from having second thoughts as she dressed Saturday morning. Hurriedly she fastened the belt on her khaki slacks and stepped into matching tennis shoes. Another prank call had interrupted her rest and she'd overslept. She gave her hair a few cursory strokes then let it hang loose, held back from her face by a pastel-print scarf knotted at her nape. The soft rose-colored sweater gave her complexion a pink glow, so she didn't bother with any makeup except for eyeliner, a little shadow, and muted pink lipstick.

The doorbell rang just as she inserted the second of the small gold earrings, causing her to drop the back. Torn between getting the door before Matt woke Lisa, and finding the earring back while she still had an idea where it might be, she muttered in exasperation and hurried to let him in.

"Hi," she whispered, "Lisa's still sleeping. Come in and I'll be ready in a second." She explained as she hastened back to her room, "I dropped the back to my earring."

She was frantically searching the top of her dresser when a deep voice whispered, "There it is." She swung around to find Matt leaning a shoulder against her bedroom door frame and pointing to a spot on the carpet at her feet. Before she could recover her composure, he stepped into her room and knelt to retrieve the small bit of metal.

Straightening slowly, he offered it to her on his open palm, humor sparkling in his eyes. The fresh scent of clean skin, starched cotton, and tangy aftershave filled Dawn's nostrils. She snatched the piece of jewelry from his hand with a murmured, "Thanks."

Leaving the mirror, she crossed the small room to gather up her purse and a lightweight jacket. When she turned Matt was still there watching her from his former position against

the door frame, one hand on his hip and the other hanging
from his back pocket by its thumb. He wore a short-sleeved
madras sport shirt neatly tucked into the waistband of a pair
of softly faded jeans.

"Ready?" he asked with a grin.

"I guess so, although I still don't think I should be going,"
she whispered.

"Why not?"

"I don't know, I just don't." She locked the apartment door
behind them.

"You're afraid to fly with me?"

"Of course not."

"You don't like Austin?" He took her elbow as they de-
scended the stairs.

"Austin is beautiful this time of year."

"Ah, then that leaves me. You don't trust me."

When she didn't answer, he laughed good-naturedly. "I
gave you my promise, remember?"

"I remember," she answered quietly, knowing she had more
to fear from herself than from the big man beside her. He
opened her car door but she hesitated, turning to look up into
his face. "Matt, do you keep your promises?"

He looked skyward then gently urged her into the car muttering, "I won't if you keep looking at me like that."

"Here, let me help you." Matt settled her in the small cock-
pit and fastened her seat belt. "Have you ever flown in a small
aircraft before?" he asked as he slipped into the pilot's seat.

"No, I haven't."

"Well, other than the obvious difference in size, you'll notice a difference in the ride, kind of like comparing a limou-
sine to a sports car. You feel the bumps in the road more in
a small car. This is the sports car," he said with a grin, fas-
tening his own belt, "only our road will be the air currents.
You'll feel the dips and bumps, and if we run across gusty
winds, you might feel them push the plane around a little,
kind of a sideways sliding sensation, but it's nothing to worry
about. Just remember, I can land this thing almost anywhere,

from a dirt road to a pasture." Matt finished his preflight check as he talked, then put away the check sheet and smiled at her. "Any questions?"

"Not a one."

"You're sure? No questions at all?"

"Matt, I have complete confidence in your abilities as a pilot." He looked taken aback by her declaration of faith so she continued, "I realize what you flew for the Army was a lot more complicated than this airplane, and that the military doesn't let just anyone pilot their expensive equipment. However," she added with a grin, "if any questions do occur, you'll be the first to know."

"You've got yourself a deal." He shook his head and chuckled, then pulled the plane onto the runway of the small suburban airport and taxied to the end of it. Revving the engine, he let off the brakes, sending the craft speeding down the blacktop, shuddering slightly as it bumped along. They were airborne in a matter of moments.

"So, you know about my military career, huh?" He glanced at her out of the corner of his eye.

She shrugged. "Not really. I know you were a helicopter pilot and that your aircraft went down, period."

"I see. And how did you come upon that bit of information, if I may ask?"

She sensed rather than heard the tension in his voice. "Lisa told me when I asked her if she knew anything about your leg injury. I wasn't sure you were telling me the truth when you said it wasn't really my fault."

He grunted noncommittally and banked the plane sharply as he took his course, tipping Dawn toward him. He leveled the aircraft again and after several moments of silence asked, "How did Lisa know? As far as I can remember, she's never worked for me, or even anyone in our section." He added in afterthought, "I never said it wasn't your fault, I just said it had been injured before."

Dawn chuckled at his disgruntled tone and his unwillingness to gracefully concede the point of their old dispute.

"Well?" he insisted.

"Well what?"

"How does Lisa know my military history?"

Dawn grinned at him. "I'm probably breaking some sort of code of the clerks in telling you this, but you, Mr. Ivans, are the topic of a lot of the conversations in our building."

He looked at her incredulously. "You're kidding!"

"Nope. Of course it's understandable when you figure you've single-handedly sent more clerks screaming into the night than Ebenezer Scrooge."

"Oh, come on," he protested.

"*And*," she continued cheerfully, warming to the topic, "you are single, not bad-looking, somewhat eccentric, and . . ."

Matt was laughing. "Enough already! Eccentric? Gee, where do you come up with this stuff?"

Dawn continued grinning in delight. "It's all true, honest. I heard every word of it in the break room." She paused and chuckled. "Or from Lisa. My first week on the job one of your former clerks even offered me sanctuary on another floor of the building in case I needed a place to hide."

"Women," Matt grumbled as he shook his head in disgust. "I'm not believing any of this."

"Why would I lie? Especially since working for you has put me on the hot line with you. When we have a, uh, difference of opinion, Lisa knows about it before the day is out. When we eat together, the news is all over the building. Believe me, when it comes to you, the gossip network in that place rivals anything I've ever seen."

"Maybe it's you everyone's interested in."

"Yeah, right." Dawn grabbed the armrest as the plane dipped then bumped a couple of times before smoothing out. "The only reason I'm of interest is because I work for Ivans the—" She stopped herself barely in time. But not soon enough, it seemed.

Matt prodded in a warning tone, "Ivans the what?"

She bit her lip and looked out the window on her right. Rolling hills undulated below them in carpets of green, splashed with patches of wildflowers. A creek threw back sparks of sunlight as it ambled through a meadow.

"Come on, Dawn, it won't be the first time I've carried an unpleasant nickname. Ivans the what?"

"I'm sorry, Matt. The girls you've scared half to death dubbed you Ivans the Terrible." She couldn't look at him. She felt absolutely wretched about the slip.

"Ivans the Terrible," he repeated thoughtfully. Then he threw his head back and laughed. "I like it. I think I'll have it put on a nameplate for my desk."

"You would," she grouched, wrinkling her nose, not sure why it bothered her that he took it so lightly.

He laughed again, a gusty sound, full of enjoyment. "It beats what some of the men in my unit used to call me."

Dawn tipped her head and scowled at him. "Which was?"

"Never mind, it's not for tender ears."

She stifled a sudden yawn and he teased, "I thought you trusted my flying. Looks like you lost some sleep worrying about it."

"Hardly. We've acquired a prank caller and last night, or rather, this morning was one of his times. He usually wakes me up between one and two-thirty."

He fixed hard eyes on her. "Have you contacted the police or the phone company?"

"No, I just hang up on him."

"Maybe you should change your number."

"If it keeps up we probably will."

"What's the nature of his calls?"

"The nature? Oh, you mean how does he act? Well, the first time he said he'd called earlier and asked where I'd been, but since then he just breathes."

"You're kidding."

"No. Pretty junior high, huh?"

"Do you think it's someone you know?"

"Now *you've* got to be kidding. I can't think of a soul who is that socially arrested."

Matt banked the small aircraft and skirted wispy tendrils of clouds as he made his descent. They touched down with less impact than the average parking lot speed bump and taxied to the apron.

Chapter Seven

The blue April sky formed an enormous canvas on which fat white clouds floated, a textured backdrop for Texas's Capitol dome. Dozens of tourists wandered the grounds, their faces hidden behind various pieces of photographic equipment as they busily snapped pictures of the immense pink granite edifice.

"Pretty impressive, huh?" Matt slanted her a grin before raising his camera and clicking off several frames.

She'd laughed when he produced a couple of guide books from behind his seat after they landed, but she'd really been surprised when he'd hauled out the large camera bag.

"I told you we'd do the tourist thing," he'd reminded her good-naturedly as he'd unlocked the door of the rental car, "and you didn't even bring a camera. But I guess you've been here before?"

"Not since I was about six years old. This is your first time, then?" she'd asked.

"Yeah, it is." Once he'd headed them in the direction of town he'd looked at her and grinned. "It's always more fun exploring new places if you have someone to share the experience with." He'd paused before adding, "That way, if you make a fool of yourself, at least you're not alone."

She'd laughed and swatted his arm. Now she sat at the base of a statue on the far end of the esplanade from the Capitol building while Matt removed the telephoto lens from his camera. He'd used it to get some shots of the ornate building's crowning glory, the Goddess of Liberty.

Dawn closed her eyes and raised her face to the sun, inhaling the sweet fragrance of the flower gardens. It was so peaceful here in spite of the dozens of people moving around them, and she couldn't ask for a more charming companion.

Ivans the Terrible, charming?

She opened her eyes and caught Matt lowering the camera, a strange, pensive look on his face. His only apology for photographing her unawares was a lopsided half grin and a shrug of one shoulder.

After touring the Capitol building, they went to the Governor's mansion and then on to the Harry Ransom Center at the University of Texas. There, a Gutenberg Bible printed in 1455 caught Dawn's interest.

"Just think," she whispered reverently, "we're actually looking at something that was printed during Christopher Columbus's childhood. Can you believe it?"

Matt was keenly interested in the photography exhibit so they decided to save the three hundred plus paintings in the Michener Collection for another time. It was after 2:00 when they finally tore themselves away from the museum.

"I'm hungry, how about you?" Matt asked.

"Starved, now that you mention it."

Finding a place to eat around a college campus hardly constituted a challenge, but deciding on which fast-food establishment to grace with their business set off a good-natured war.

"Fish?" he offered.

"Yuck, Matt they deep fry it in grease, then pour on more grease for good measure. It's suicide!"

"But it tastes good."

"How about tacos?"

"You'd eat tacos from an assembly line when you live in the heart of homemade territory?"

"Hmm, you have a point. After Maria's they'd be a letdown, wouldn't they."

"Without a doubt. Pizza?"

"More grease and fat and cholesterol and—"

"Okay, okay, I get the picture." Matt slung his arm around her neck and squeezed slightly in a mock stranglehold. "Gee, what a nag. You'd think I was eighty years old and on a respirator."

"Keep eating like that and you'll be a forty-year-old in need of bypass surgery," she returned with a soft punch to his solid midsection.

"Aw, I didn't know you cared."

"I don't, I'd just hate to have to break in a new boss."

"Yeah, sure. Okay, how about hamburgers if we skip the French fries and have diet soda instead of milkshakes."

She thought a moment, then nodded slowly. "That would work." But when they stepped up to the counter at the hamburger stand, Dawn, with a straight face, ordered a mushroom cheeseburger with bacon, a large side of fries, and a strawberry milkshake.

Matt's jaw dropped and he stared at her dumbfounded. Causally, she turned and looked up at him, her expression one of total innocence. He didn't hold back, he threw back his head and roared, his laughter drawing the attention of everyone in the place. An embarrassed flush climbed her face and still he laughed. Finally, exasperated, she turned to the girl behind the counter.

"Give him the same, but make it a double burger and a large chocolate shake, please." Then she tipped up her chin and stalked to a booth in the corner, acting as if she had no idea who Matt might be.

Still chuckling, Matt followed behind her. He dropped into the booth, reached across the table, and grabbed her hand. "Dawn, I—" He stopped abruptly, horrified. He'd been about to say, *Dawn, I love you.* Well, he thought with surprise, maybe he did. But for now he grinned and shook his head. "Dawn, I'm glad you came."

She smiled serenely. "Me, too."

Ater lunch, they took the sightseeing excursion on Town Lake. Standing at the rail of the paddle-wheeled boat in companionable silence, it seemed perfectly natural when Matt slipped his arm around her waist. She leaned against his side, her arms resting on the wide wooden rail in front of her.

Tuning out the tour guide's monologue, she enjoyed the feel of the breeze that gently lifted her hair, the vibration of the deck under her feet as the boat's big wheel churned the water, the pressure of Matt's arm, firm and protective. She didn't need a man to take care of her, she really didn't, but it felt so good standing close against Matt's solid body. Comfortable. *Secure.* She straightened.

An elderly couple asked Matt to take their picture with their camera, then offered to do the same for him and Dawn.

"Come over here," he instructed, pulling her hand. He stood against the wheelhouse under the boat's name and arranged her in front of him, his arms around her waist. "Now say cheese."

Dawn laughed and covered his arms with her own as they posed for their picture.

"You two been going together long?" the old woman asked.

He felt Dawn stiffen in his arms, but gave her a gentle squeeze in warning and replied, "Not long."

The woman winked at Dawn and said, "Well, I'm here to tell you it gets better with every day."

Her husband quit fiddling with the camera's focus ring long enough to give her a loving smile. "Yup, that's for sure."

"Wilbur and I have been married forty-seven years."

"You don't say," Matt exclaimed.

The older couple beamed proudly. "We surely do say," Wilbur answered. "Forty-seven years ago today I did the smartest thing I've ever done in my life."

"Oh, Papa," his wife demurred, a flush climbing her wrinkled cheeks. But Matt noticed that her eyes sparkled like a young girl's. His arms tightened again as Wilbur depressed the shutter release. But why? To warn Dawn to play along for the old folks' sake, or to warn himself not to let her go?

The scene on the boat had made Dawn skittish, teasing her

with thoughts of what it might be like to make a home again. A home with Matt. She had to forcefully remind herself that her focus had changed. She no longer wanted that kind of life.

They wandered through the shops on Old Pecan Street. Matt took her hand as they exited a small gallery and swung it lazily between them as they strolled along the storefronts.

He paused at a window of silver jewelry. "Let's go in here."

They laughed together at some of the whimsical creations. They were on their way back out the door when he stopped. "That one," he said to the clerk, pointing to a silver heart done in delicate filigree. He paid for his purchase, but when the clerk reached for a sheet of tissue to wrap it, Matt held out an open palm. "No, I'll take that."

He turned to Dawn, the necklace between his hands, and said softly, "May I?"

Her heart took its predictable leap at the honeyed tone and her mouth went dry. His eyes were as warm as his voice. "I . . ." she stammered. "You didn't need to—"

"I know." He held up the ends of the black velvet cord and she turned obediently around, lifting her hair out of the way.

His touch sent shivers down her arms and spine and she very badly wanted to lean back against his warmth. She closed her eyes and swallowed hard, fighting her response to the feather light brush of his fingertips. *Stop this*, she ordered her rebellious senses. *Stop it right now!*

Matt dropped his hands and stepped back. "There."

She touched the pendant and whispered, "Thank you, it's beautiful."

Their eyes met and held for a minute, then Matt, again wearing that pensive look from earlier in the day, shoved his hands in his pockets and nodded toward the street. "Your turn to pick the restaurant."

They walked slowly, not touching now, as the light faded into evening. She chose an informal open-fronted eatery specializing in Italian food. They took a table near the sidewalk where they could watch the people passing by as they ate their veal parmesan.

The day was coming to an end, and suddenly it seemed

they had nothing to say. Or was it, Dawn wondered, that they didn't *need* to say anything?

Their conversation on the flight home consisted of forced and broken phrases. Sentiments concisely expressed, Dawn thought, in futile attempts to bridge the self-consciousness that had sprung up between them.

"The weather certainly cooperated today."

"Didn't it though." Matt nodded toward his side window. "Look at that sunset."

She leaned forward a little. "Beautiful."

"The veal was good."

"Very. I ate too much."

"Umm, me too."

The aircraft took one of those little sideways slides Matt had mentioned and Dawn's stomach followed suit. Both dipped back the other way a bit and she visualized the way a kite dances in the air.

"Okay?" Matt asked.

"Just fine," she assured him.

After a while Matt pointed to two thick sprinklings of lights ahead of and below them. "There's home," he said, referring to the Dallas–Fort Worth metroplex.

At her apartment, he walked her to the door. Fishing for her key in the dark, she said, "I really had a great time today. Thanks for taking me."

"You're welcome, but don't you think you should look a man in the eye when you thank him?"

Her heart skipped a beat and her hand fell still in the jumbled interior of her purse. She glanced up at him, flashed a quick grin, and resumed her hunt. "Sorry, the thanks is genuine, but I think I should have looked for my key before we got out of the car."

"Here." Matt held a miniature flashlight he kept on his key chain over her open purse.

"There it is." Dawn flashed him another quick grin then inserted her key in the door.

"Now you can look me in the eye," he murmured, stopping her flight with a hand on her arm.

She swallowed, moistened her lips, and took a deep breath. Her lungs filled with his tangy scent. She leaned imperceptibly toward him. Pasting on a fake smile, she looked up into his eyes. "I had a wonderful time, Matt, I really mean it. It was like a mini-vacation. Thank you."

His hand cupped the side of her face and her heart did a back flip. "Matt," she protested, her voice a rasped plea for mercy.

"You're right," he agreed, his voice low and seductive, "it wasn't a good idea last time either, was it?"

Mutely, Dawn shook her head.

"But I wouldn't have missed it for the world," he whispered as he bent to her mouth. He brushed her lips lightly with his own, then pulled back, running the pad of his thumb over her lower lip. He didn't hold her, didn't touch her except for his hand cradling her face.

"Matt, you promised." Her breathy tones slid over Matt's skin like electrical impulses, sending his heart leaping in his chest. Again she'd voiced a plea. Not an accusation. Not a denial.

His voice quiet, coaxing, he murmured, "The day is over and so's the trip. Didn't I keep my promise?" He would leave the decision with her.

She didn't answer, didn't move away, just stood there with eyes wide and breath racing. So he folded her more securely in his arms and kissed her gently but thoroughly.

When the kiss ended, he dropped his forehead to hers and drew a deep breath. She smelled of warm spring air, of Italian spices, of honeysuckle, of Dawn. Her small hands were pressed against his chest. He covered the one over his heart with one of his own, flattening her palm. He knew she could feel the hammering through his chest wall.

He brushed her lips lightly with his one last time and whispered gruffly, "You'd better go in now."

Oh, Lord, it had happened again! She should never have gone with him; she knew all along it would be a mistake. She knew better, she *knew* better!

Dawn lay in her bed, castigating herself as the tears ran unchecked to soak into her pillow. Her misery wouldn't let her hide from the awful truth. She wanted Matt Ivans. She wanted him to belong to her more than she ever thought it possible for one person to want another, more than she could remember ever wanting her young husband.

All Matt had to do to set her mind to reeling was simply to take her in his arms. To make her lose all track of time and place, he had only to kiss her. In less than thirty seconds he could make her forget all her stern resolves, all the pain of her past. He could do all that with only a kiss.

The telephone rang. She didn't want to answer. It was too early for their annoying caller. Probably a wrong number, but with Lisa still out, she couldn't take the chance of not answering. Her sister might need her. She padded into the living room, sniffled, then lifted the receiver. "Hello."

"I hope I didn't wake you. I just had to hear your voice again before I went to sleep."

"Matt?"

"Who else?"

He sounded incredibly weary. It must be her state of mind. Against her will, she expressed her concern for him. "Are you all right?"

"Not really."

"What's wrong? What happened?"

"You." She heard him sigh heavily. "You happened, Dawn."

She wiped her eyes on the sleeve of her nightshirt. "I . . . I don't know what you're talking about."

"Yes, you do," he chided gently. "Straight talk, remember? Keep it simple and honest."

"Matt, I . . ." She couldn't finish the thought, didn't know what to say.

"You what, Dawn? You enjoy being with me? You like my kisses? You miss me? What?"

"I just . . . I don't know." She grasped the receiver with both hands. "Matt, I can't do this."

"You can't *not* do this. Dawn, magic happens when we're together and you know it."

She didn't answer.

"Don't you, Dawn?" he insisted gently.

A quivering sigh shimmied through her body and in a small defeated voice she admitted, "Yes, I know it."

"I want to come over later. We need to talk."

"No, Matt, please. I told you I can't do this and I mean it."

"Then that's what we need to talk about."

"No."

"Dawn, is there someone else?"

A short, sarcastic laugh. "No, no one else, Matt."

"Then I'll see you around eleven. Good night, sweetheart."

"No, Matt—"

But he'd hung up.

Matt lay with one arm flung over his eyes, his other hand resting on the phone. He'd fought valiantly with himself over whether to place this call, and his better sense had lost out.

It was too late to back down now. He'd declared himself, though he'd had no intention of doing it so soon. Dawn didn't seem very receptive to the idea, but that didn't bother him. The hard part was over—he'd admitted to himself that he loved her. After that, convincing her they belonged together should be a snap. *Should be.*

Matt knocked on the apartment door at 11:00 sharp.

Lisa answered, but hung onto the partially open door, blocking his entrance. "Hello, Mr. Ivans."

He nodded curtly. "I'd like to see Dawn, please."

"I'm sorry, she's not in right now."

Matt didn't believe her. He pushed firmly on the door, moving Dawn's sister back into the room, then stalked to Dawn's bedroom without a word. He returned a moment later to stand, hands on his hips, surveying the apartment. He eyed another closed door, Lisa's room he surmised, and started for it.

"She's not in there either, but you're welcome to look."

He scowled at the girl leaning against the edge of the open front door. She reminded him of her stubborn sister, standing there with her arms crossed and her chin tilted up at a defiant angle. He changed direction and went to stand in front of her. Giving her his most intimidating frown, he growled, "Where is she, Lisa? We have some talking to do and I mean to find her."

Lisa dropped her eyes and shifted her weight nervously from one foot to the other, then pierced him with a hard look of her own. "What do you want to talk to her about?"

"That's none of your business."

"Oh, but it is. You see"—Lisa paused to swallow—"I'm the one responsible for her being here. I sent her the application and urged her to move in with me. It's my fault she's working for you."

"Fair enough." Too occupied by his campaign to win Dawn to take insult at Lisa's opinion of him as an employer, he assured, "My intentions toward your sister are serious and honorable, if that's what you're worried about."

Instead of being relieved as he'd expected, Lisa dropped her arms and moaned, "I was afraid something like this would happen." She looked up at him, imploringly, again reminding him of the woman he'd come here to see. "Please, Mr. Ivans, leave her alone, you'll only make her miserable. She doesn't deserve this, she's been through enough already."

Alarm flared through him at Lisa's distress. He took hold of the girl's arms and demanded, "Lisa, tell me where she is. She's all right, isn't she?"

"Yes, yes, she's fine. She just doesn't want to talk to you."

"Okay," he said slowly, relieved. "She doesn't have to talk then, she can just listen, but I've got to see her."

"Mr. Ivans, please, I've told you she doesn't want—"

He dropped her arms and turned away, running a hand through his hair in frustration. "Confound it, woman, I'm in love with your sister! I have to see her, I have to tell her!"

"You . . . you're in love with Dawn?"

"Yes." Matt wearily rubbed his eyes, eyes which he'd

barely closed all night long as he lay in his bed sorting things through.

"You're sure about this?"

"Where is she, Lisa?" he asked, a note of warning in his voice.

Lisa bit her lip again, obviously torn by indecision. She glanced toward the drapes covering the balcony door.

Matt followed her gaze and raised his eyebrows in silent query. She lifted her chin that annoying little notch and plopped down on the sofa, arms crossed belligerently. He smiled his thanks and quickly crossed to the glass doors. Pushing aside the curtain he eased the door open. Dawn stood with her back to him, arms crossed at her waist.

"Is he gone?" she asked softly.

"No, he doesn't discourage that easily," came his equally soft reply.

"I was afraid of that." She answered without turning around.

"Why? What are you afraid of, sweetheart?" He moved up behind her and cupped her shoulders.

"You."

Her hair smelled so sweet, so fresh. He laid his cheek against her head, luxuriating in the silky texture, and whispered, "There's nothing to be afraid of. I'm mostly bellow and bluff and you know it."

"Yes, I do know it and that's what frightens me."

"Would it help to know I love you?"

She paused. "No, that only makes it worse."

Not the response Matt expected. His voice sharpened. "How so?"

"It tempts me to let my guard down, and I can't do that."

He turned her to face him. "Of course you can. I would never hurt you."

"Maybe you would, maybe you wouldn't, but I'm not willing to take that chance. I've worked too hard getting where I am to risk it."

"And *where*, exactly, are you?" Fear gave his voice a derisive edge.

His tone made Dawn angry. "I'm where I want to be! I'm building a life away from my childhood home, I'm meeting people, I'm becoming a person I like and respect, and I have a decent job, although it looks like that will change. I'm my own person. I'm free, Matt, and I won't let anyone, *anyone* jeopardize that for me!"

She twisted from him, presenting her back as she gripped the iron railing and fought against tears. Matt said he loved her, her heart soared at the words, but she couldn't let him! She couldn't let herself. *Not again, please Lord, not again.*

Matt's hands closed almost painfully around her shoulders and his voice snapped like a whip. "And freedom is more important to you than love, is that it?"

On a trembling breath she whispered, "Yes, that's it."

His hands fell away but his voice flailed her again, "Then I guess you're right, we have nothing to talk about. I had no idea you were so driven. With such single-mindedness, you should go far. As soon as there's an opening elsewhere, I'll approve your transfer."

Trembling, she stood silent, tense, waiting for the next verbal lash to fall, waiting for him to take the proverbial pound of flesh in retaliation for his wounded pride, but all was quiet. He'd gone and already she felt the loss.

Matt crossed the small apartment in a few angry strides. Lisa waylaid him at the door. "Mr. Ivans, try to understand, Dawn's had a rough time."

He cut her off with a curt, "Haven't we all?" and slammed the door behind him.

The sound echoed through the apartment as Lisa stared at the door. Stricken, she turned toward the balcony just as Dawn stepped through the curtain, her shoulders slumped, her face ashen.

"Dawn, I—" She was silenced by a raised hand.

Dawn eased across the apartment as though walking on splintered glass, her arms crossed protectively at her waist, moving carefully as if she herself might shatter at the least noise, the least contact. Reaching the sanctuary of her room, she quietly closed the door behind her and Lisa didn't see her for the rest of the day.

Matt headed his Firebird out the old highway and opened it up, its twin exhaust pipes roaring his hurt and fury into the spring air. The car tore along between pastures gilded with black-eyed Susans and dotted with grazing cattle, hugging the turns like it was melded to the road. On the straight-aways, cushions of buttercups softened the edges of the pavement, but Matt didn't see them as he pushed harder, going faster, taking more chances.

He knew he'd come close to being airborne when he crested those last two hills, but he didn't care. Why should he care? Dawn didn't. The only woman in his entire thirty-two years he'd ever said "I love you" to, and she didn't care.

Screaming tires bit into the pavement then churned up a hail of gravel and dust when he down-shifted and whipped the car off the road into the dirt parking lot of a roadside bar. He slammed the car door behind him and bounded up the wooden steps, shoving his way into the ice house with more force than necessary.

The doors flapped behind him and the proprietor eyed him warily. " 'Lo, Matt. Ain't seen you in a while," he greeted in a voice much like stones rolling inside a tin can.

Matt didn't bother to acknowledge the greeting. "Whiskey, double."

"How much you had so far?"

"None, not that it's any of your business. Now are you going to serve me or do I go elsewhere?"

"Wouldn't want to lose the business," the old man replied amiably as he continued to dry a glass, "but the condition of my patrons *is* my concern according to the law."

Matt sighed. "I know. Sorry. Get me the whiskey, okay?"

"Sure, just surprised me is all. As much time as you used to spend here shootin' pool, I've never seen you drink the hard stuff. Anything you want to talk about?"

Matt dropped onto a barstool and let his head fall back on his shoulders. Closing his eyes he gave a snort of dry laughter then looked at the rotund man behind the bar. "Bartenders and barbers, the working man's psychiatrists."

"Yeah, but ain't too many barbers around anymore. Ya gotta go to a 'stylist' to get a trim these days." He set a drink down in front of Matt, a single shot. "Girl trouble?"

"How'd you guess?" Matt turned the glass in his fingers, watching the lights dance in the golden liquid.

"Because I ain't never seen you this riled, and I never knowed you to be a man to fool around, so I figger it's serious."

"Serious? It could be, but she's not interested. Her job, *her freedom,* are more important." Matt downed the drink. "This time make it a double like I asked you to."

"What you need is somethin' to eat. How 'bout a burger?"

Matt glared at the man a moment then groused, "Oh all right, but I'd rather have something with a little more punch to it. Got any of your chili?"

"Yeah, but it might be a couple a days old."

"That's fine," Matt retorted. "I feel like living dangerously."

He dropped some quarters into the jukebox and selected the most depressing country songs he could find, then nursed a bottle of cola while waiting on his lunch. The bartender was right. Getting drunk wouldn't solve a thing.

"Here ya go." The chili arrived, bubbling and aromatic, topped with shredded cheese and chopped onions. The proprietor left him to his musical laments and brooding thoughts.

Matt finished his meal and rose to pull his wallet from his pocket. "Thanks," he said, "that hit the spot after all."

The old man grinned and set down the glass he'd been polishing. "Thought it might," he agreed.

Matt paid his tab and slid his wallet back into his hip pocket. "But what do I do about the girl?"

The round belly wobbled and the laughter rolled. "Boy, if I knew the answer to that, I'd be a rich man. But tell you what, give 'er some time to get used to the idea. Maybe you just surprised 'er is all. Can't imagine any girl turning down a fine feller like you."

By the time he reached home, Matt knew he'd pushed his luck too far.

Chapter Eight

Head pounding and stomach tied in knots, Dawn made her way to her desk. She'd wanted to stay home but managed to convince herself that grown women didn't hide from their problems; they faced them as best they could and moved on. And she'd have to move on, just as soon as there was an opening. If nothing came soon here at the bank, she would look elsewhere. She passed Lilly in the hall.

"Hey, Dawn," the girl greeted, cracking the ever-present chewing gum, "you look rough. You feeling okay?"

Dawn waved noncommittally and kept walking. Oh great, she'd hardly slept since Friday night and it showed. Matt would be sure to comment. *One day at a time, Dawn, or just minute to minute if it comes to that. Taken in small doses you can get through anything.*

Matt wasn't at his desk. It didn't even look as if he'd come in yet today. She performed her morning routine, thankful for the mindless repetition, except that she didn't fill Matt's coffee cup. His phone rang constantly, the calls rotating to other loan agents when his number remained unanswered.

At 9:45 her phone rang. Matt's supervisor told her Matt wouldn't be in today and to divide the applications she processed among three of the other agents. With a fleeting sense of satisfaction she wondered if Matt was the one hiding.

Lisa called a short while later to check on her.

"I'm fine, thanks. Matt isn't here."

"He's not?"

"No, and Lisa, I don't think I need to remind you that this is not a public matter."

"Of course not!"

"Just making sure. Not even to your best friend, and I mean it."

"Dawn, *you* are my best friend. I wouldn't do that to you."

"Okay, sorry." Dawn sighed. "I feel like death warmed over. It's a blessing he isn't here today."

"I know," Lisa sympathized. "He must be feeling just as bad to have stayed home."

"Sure, and pigs fly."

"Doubtful, isn't it?" Lisa muttered.

"It is. Well, got to get busy. Thanks for checking on me though, I appreciate it."

She hung up, wondering for the first time just how Matt did feel about their scene in the light of a new day. But thinking about it only made her head begin pounding again.

In the middle of the afternoon, a quiet little thought came creeping. *You hurt him.*

I what?

You hurt him, her conscience repeated. *He came to tell you he loved you and you said you didn't care.*

I didn't say that.

That's what he heard and you know it.

But I do care, you know I do. I just can't let myself get caught up again.

You could. Do you plan to go the rest of your life without love?

I can't take the kind of pain love brings, not again. I don't have the strength to survive it a second time.

What about the pain you were in yesterday, are in today, and will probably be in tomorrow? You wouldn't be suffering now if you'd just told him that you love him too.

I don't know if I love him.

Yeah, right.

Desire and love are not necessarily the same thing.

If it's just desire, then why are you so miserable?

And who's to say it wouldn't get worse if I were to go to him?

Sick as a dog, Matt knew he'd come close to needing hospitalization. Food poisoning could be fatal. He wondered idly as he rubbed his sore stomach with one hand and pressed his aching temple with the other, if a broken heart could be fatal too, or if it was only the stupid things it drove a man to do. Like driving too fast, downing suspect chili, little things like that.

He'd barely been able to call the office this morning. Now, though, he was in much better shape. He could hardly drag himself to his feet, but he could see across the room. When it wasn't spinning. Yep, much better shape. If it weren't so painful, he'd laugh.

He might try talking some sense into himself, but the effort required for such a speech exceeded his ability to produce it, so forget that. In fact, thinking took more energy than he was capable of sustaining right now, so he closed his eyes and slipped back into that semiconscious state that passed for sleep. Not true sleep, because the pain in his head and stomach were too sharp to allow him that deep a rest. If he were still alive come tomorrow morning, he'd try thinking again then.

Matt didn't return to work Tuesday, either. Dawn heard mention of a stomach virus and supposed that explained his absence. She felt guilty about it, but not having Matt there made things much easier for her. Jerry called in the afternoon, asking her out for Friday night.

"Come on, Dawn, three weeks is a long time to put a guy off. Let's go dancing with Doug and Lisa; they could use chaperoning."

She sincerely did not want to go. Right now she didn't care if she ever got near another man, but maybe spending time in the company of Lisa's friends would take the edge off this dull ache. "All right, but I doubt Doug will thank you for it."

She could hear the smile in his voice as Jerry agreed, "No,

probably not, but what are buddies for if not to harass? Pick you up about seven-thirty."

Dawn caught herself smiling when she hung up. Jerry was amusing to talk to, and pleasant enough to be with, and that's what she needed. A man she didn't take seriously, a man who could entertain her, but who would never touch her heart. Unconsciously, her eyes strayed to Matt's empty chair.

At home, Matt struggled to sit up in bed. He was thirsty and he needed to go to the bathroom. Gingerly he scooted up a few inches against the headboard, rested, then moved a few more. So far so good. The head still ached, but no longer felt as if it'd been cleaved with an axe. Slowly, he eased his legs over the side of the mattress, pausing until the wave of nausea passed.

His feet touched the floor. Steadying himself with a hand on the bed, he straightened an inch at a time. *Slowly now, slowly.* He made it! Standing up straight and on his own two feet! *Take it easy; don't rush or you'll never get there. One shuffling step at a time, that's right, that's right. Turn on the bathroom light. Ow!*

Squinting, he looked in the mirror. Corpses looked better than he did. Skin a pasty gray, the two day's growth of stubble enhanced his derelict appearance. Dark circles underscored his eyes and deep furrows lined his cheeks. That blasted woman had aged him fifty years in just two days!

He turned on the tap and splashed his face several times, then filled a glass and rinsed his mouth before drinking deeply. His mouth tasted sour and in general he felt like a dirty dish-rag, but realized he didn't smell nearly that good.

Thoroughly disgusted with himself, he stripped off the clothes he'd been wearing since Sunday morning and turned on the shower. He lathered his abused body, washing away the stench of illness, then worked a generous dollop of sham-poo through his greasy hair. When it was finally washed and rinsed to the squeaking-clean stage, he stood under the refresh-ing spray until the water began to run cool.

He emerged feeling a little more human. He took a swig of

mouthwash, gargled, swished and spit, then knotted a towel around his waist and made his way to the kitchen to rehydrate himself.

A quart of apple juice later, Matt felt reasonably certain he would live. He sat at the table nibbling on crackers and re-playing Sunday's scene in his mind.

His mind! He snorted at the thought. *What mind? You lost it over that woman! You're a chump, Ivans.*

He stood abruptly and had to grab the table when his legs wobbled under him. Enough of this! He was back in control—well, almost—and tomorrow he would be back on the job. No little dab of femininity was going to get the best of him.

So she turned him down, big deal. No shame in that. The shame would have been in lacking the courage to go to her. And he'd done that. He'd laid it on the line. The lady simply wasn't interested. Now he'd resume his life the way it had been before she'd turned it upside down.

Before he'd ever kissed her.

Before he'd ever laid eyes on her.

Life before Dawn?

He wasn't sure he could remember it.

"Gawd, Matt, you look awful!"

"Thanks, Jim, it's always good to get an honest opinion."

Dawn's heart made a little leap at the sound of his voice, and relief that he was back lifted a weight from her shoulders she hadn't known she carried. But then she saw him.

If she hadn't overheard Jim's remark before seeing Matt for herself, she might have blurted out something equally as tact-less. As it happened, she felt the urge to throw her arms around him and cry. He looked terrible! Pale and drawn, he'd obviously been very ill and still hadn't fully recovered.

Matt glanced up to find Dawn staring at him, mouth slightly agape. Surely she didn't think she'd run him out of his own office? His eyes fastened on her lips. Moist, soft . . .

Get on with life, that's what he had to do. He nodded curtly to her and turned away, his only greeting a sharp, "Ms. Mil-ler."

Her eyes widened in momentary surprise and she murmured, "Good to see you back, Mr. Ivans."

Their day progressed much like their first week together. Dawn seemed stiff and uncomfortable under his unyielding standards, but that was no fault of his. She wanted her career? Fine, she could perform her job like a professional. No more Mr. Nice Guy, he had certain expectations of anyone working for him and she could either meet them or get out. He wasn't cutting her any more slack.

In fact, he'd tried to raise his voice to her once, but winced in pain and stopped mid-sentence. At the end of the day, Matt waited until Dawn was out of sight to close up his own desk, then merged with the stream of people leaving the building. He didn't have the heart for his usual long hours today.

In the parking lot, he discovered Lisa's car sat only two spaces over from his. He couldn't help overhearing her talking to her sister as he unlocked his door.

"When Doug called today he said you and Jerry were joining us Friday night at the Corral. Why didn't you tell me?"

Dawn slid into the car and Matt couldn't hear her reply. He supposed the Corral was the Old Oak Corral where he'd seen Dawn with Lisa and her friends. Well, let the cowboy have her if he could get her. With freedom being her number-one priority, Matt doubted anyone was going to interest her for long.

He threw his briefcase into the seat with enough force to send it bouncing into the floor board. Just let her wrap that cocky tinhorn around her little finger, it'd serve him right. He slammed the car door and snaked the seat belt across his body. That cowboy was not the type to put up with female shenanigans. They would probably be butting heads in no time. He turned the key and the engine roared to life.

He could imagine Dawn toe to toe with the big stocky brute: the man's face red with fury and Dawn's eyes flashing fire as she propped those tiny fists on her hips. Something twisted in his chest.

She could be a hellion all right, but he'd bet his classic car she'd be just as passionate making up. After all, he'd held her

. . . kissed her. A vision of Dawn in the husky man's arms brought an ache to Matt's gut and a dark scowl to his face. On second thought, he mused, that wouldn't do, that wouldn't do at all.

"Dawn, what are you wearing tonight? I think I'll wear jeans with my black shirt."

"What black shirt?" Dawn asked absently.

"The one with the red roses embroidered in the yokes."

"Oh, that one."

"Do you think I should wear something else?"

"No, why?"

"Well, you sounded as if you don't like it or something."

"I'm sorry. I'm just tired, I wish I could get out of going tonight."

"Dawn," Lisa whined in a singsong voice, bringing the desired chuckle from her older sister.

"Okay, okay. I'm headed for the shower now." She really did wish she could just stay home. The last three days working with Matt had been awful; the emotional strain left her completely exhausted.

She missed talking to him, laughing with him, having him for a friend. Why couldn't men ever just be friends with a woman? Dawn stared into her closet, not caring what she wore. She reached for the nearest western shirt and a pair of brown jeans and tossed them on her bed, then headed for the bathroom.

Lisa and Doug were already gone and Dawn knew Jerry would be at the door shortly. She tugged on her boots, and saw they needed polishing. Oh well, no one would notice. She stood and stomped her feet to make her jeans fall in place over the tops of the boots, then grabbed up her hairbrush.

She paused as she looked in the mirror. Was it really only six days ago that she was hurrying to get ready for a date with Matt? It seemed like another lifetime. She missed him. They'd been together the last three days, for eight hours each day, but things were no longer the same and she missed him.

You made your choice. It's what you wanted, now get over it!

Giving her hair a half dozen quick strokes, she tossed down the brush. Lipstick, eyeshadow, earrings—she was as ready as she intended to get. Stuffing the essentials in a small tooled leather handbag, she cast one last glance in her mirror.

Matt straddled a stool at the far end of the bar, lazily scanning the crowd. 10:30 and the place was packed. Tipping up the bottle, he took a small sip of cola. His eyes paused at each stocky man wearing a black hat, moving on only when he'd verified the woman at that man's side or in his arms wasn't Dawn.

After nearly half an hour, he spotted them as Jerry walked Dawn to the dance floor. She really looked good tonight. Her hair was completely free—he winced, realizing he'd come to hate that word—and swinging around her face. She wore brown jeans topped by a fitted shirt of brown plaid, generously shot through with gold thread. A gold-trimmed belt circled her small waist.

She looked great. He wet his lips with another sip of the now-warm beverage. Just then, Jerry wrapped a meaty arm around Dawn's waist and pulled her to him.

Matt was halfway off the stool before he realized it. Slowly he sank back down and took another sip of soda.

Easy boy, you've got to keep your cool. She's just a pretty lady, like a hundred others here tonight. You have to keep an emotional distance if you're going to do this.

Yeah, right. Having thus advised himself, Matt settled back to watch Dawn. Shafts of light from the mirrored ball over the dance floor reflected off the gold in her shirt and gleamed in the gold of her hair. He remembered the smell of that thick silken mane and frowned.

The band started another slow song and Jerry kept Dawn on the dance floor. Matt finished his drink, then stood and smiled to himself. Time to put Plan B into action. He carefully threaded through the dancing couples until he stood behind

Jerry. Tapping firmly on a husky shoulder, he inquired pleasantly, "May I cut in?"

Dawn's eyes flew wide at the sound of his voice and Jerry's head snapped around in equal surprise.

Men didn't usually try to cut in on another man's dance in a place like this. Fights started that way. And the look in Jerry's eye told Matt the younger man would very much like to throw a punch.

Matt stood there smiling pleasantly. "I'll bring her back, I promise."

Jerry glanced at Dawn then stepped back with a marked lack of good grace as Matt took his place.

"You look very nice tonight." It came out sounding like an accusation. Oh well, let her wonder.

"Thank you."

"Having a good time?"

"I suppose so," she answered cautiously.

"You don't sound very enthusiastic."

"I'm just tired."

"Maybe you should have stayed home." Matt held her at a most proper distance from his body.

"Maybe I should have."

"The cowboy would have been awfully disappointed, though."

"I don't think he'd have been lonely for long."

Matt chuckled softly. "Probably not. There are plenty of ladies to pick from tonight."

"Yes, there are, so I'm wondering, why are you dancing with me?" There was a touch of impatience in her voice.

Matt looked into her eyes for several heartbeats before he let the ghost of a smile touch his lips. "I think you know the answer to that." Then he closed the distance between them with a gentle pressure on her back.

When the music ended, he stopped right in front of Jerry. Stepping back, he passed Dawn's hand over to her date with a smile. "Thank you for the dance, Ms. Miller," he said, then looked Jerry in the eye and finished with extreme politeness, "and thank you for sharing her."

He resumed his watch from the corner barstool. Several times during the next hour Dawn's eyes sought him out. Sometimes he would smile at her, other times he pretended not to notice. Shortly after midnight, he slipped out and went home.

"Doug said Mr. Ivans put in an appearance at the Corral last night."

"That's right."

"Jerry was pretty ticked that he cut in on him."

"I thought he might be."

"Dawn, what's going on?"

Dawn threw the dustcloth at the endtable and flopped down on the sofa. "I wish I knew, Lissy." She lay her head back and closed her eyes before repeating softly, "I really wish I knew. I had the feeling that he was toying with me."

"How do you mean?"

"I don't know, like he was playing a game." Dawn pushed herself to her feet. "Let's finish here and find something fun to do."

"Shopping!"

Dawn moaned theatrically.

Another Monday. Well, Dawn thought, this week couldn't be any worse than last. Actually, she looked forward to getting to work. Matt was obviously up to something and she couldn't wait to see what he would do next. She soon found out.

"Good morning, Ms. Miller, new outfit?"

Unusually pleasant, but very businesslike. Okay, she could do that. "Good morning, Mr. Ivans, yes it is, do you like it?" She glanced down at her new pale-yellow suit.

"It's very nice; that's a good color for you."

Dawn struggled to keep from laughing, but silently vowed she would play along if it killed her. Removing her jacket she revealed a crepe blouse printed with watercolor tulips in shades of softest pink, yellow, and green. Matt glanced up as she turned around and a huge grin spread across his face, but for the life of her, Dawn couldn't imagine why.

She returned with his coffee and Matt smiled up at her and thanked her graciously. She smiled in return, thinking that her face was going to be awfully tired by the end of the day at this rate.

Three days later, Matt's excruciatingly polite and cheerful behavior had Dawn's nerves worn thin. It was almost as bad as having him not speak to her at all, but not quite. It confused her that, even though he did speak to her often and easily now, she felt hurt somehow. She disconsolately pulled a brush through her hair, readying herself for bed.

In the next room, Lisa talked with Doug on the phone, as she did for about an hour and a half every evening after work. Dawn couldn't ever remember being that in love.

"Dawn?" Lisa called from the next room. "The gang's getting together at Fast Freddie's this Saturday night, and we want you to come with us, okay?"

"I guess so." She'd given up resisting Lisa's efforts to get her out more. Besides, even though Jerry would no doubt be there, she wouldn't be his date if she went as part of the gang, and he'd have no excuse for his usual possessive attitude.

She didn't have anything against him, really, just his overbearing manner. *And Matt Ivans isn't?*

She ignored the little voice. Jerry was polite enough and gentlemanly, but heavily into macho attitudes, and that annoyed her.

And Ivans, of the "barefoot and pregnant" school of thought, is a now kind of guy? Come on, Dawn, admit it. Jerry just doesn't light you up like Matt does, that's the only difference.

Shut up!

Matt's saccharine smiles and droll pleasantries continued to plague her through Thursday and Friday, so she greeted the end of her work week with pleasure.

"Big plans for the weekend?"

The unexpected question startled Dawn, making her jump a little. "No, nothing out of the ordinary."

"You're not seeing Jerry?"

"It's possible, I suppose," she hedged, tidying up her desk

and quickly gathering up her things in order to make a hasty retreat.

"Well, maybe I'll see you around, then." Matt grinned at her frown.

"Good night, Mr. Ivans, have a nice weekend." *I won't let him get to me. I will NOT let him get to me.*

"Good night, Ms. Miller, I certainly plan to." Matt smiled to himself, inordinately pleased that it had finally occurred to him to use the office grapevine for his own benefit.

Fast Freddie's was touted as a family establishment. That translated to: most women would not be unduly offended by the place or its atmosphere. There were humorous signs admonishing men to mind their language and manners, and anyone who overindulged was firmly escorted from the premises. One section, raised and edged with a spooled railing, was devoted to pool tables, the other area encompassed a dance floor, jukebox, bar, small disc-jockey station, and several small tables with chairs.

Doug and Lisa's group had three of the pool tables tied up and four of the tables in the lounge area. Doug had tried to teach Dawn how to shoot, but she became self-conscious and quit when the place began filling.

She and Billy Johnson were dancing when Jerry came in looking for her. He stalked across the dance floor and cut in on the younger man with far less courtesy than Matt had used, taking Dawn roughly in his arms.

"Sorry I'm late," he greeted sarcastically, "but when I went to pick you up, nobody answered."

Dawn raised her chin as her eyes narrowed on him, replying in the same sugary tone she'd used with Matt all week, "I do beg your pardon, but I don't recall making any such arrangements."

Jerry looked a little embarrassed, but quickly recovered. "Well, you should have known I'd be along. I picked you up last week, didn't I?"

"Yes, but we had a date last week. Tonight my plans were

to join Lisa and Doug when they met a group of their friends, which I did."

"Oh, come on Dawn, you know doggone well you and I . . ." He faltered when a look of menace hardened her delicate features. Uncertainly, he finished, "I mean, everyone knows you're with me."

"They know nothing of the sort, Jerry Stevens, because it isn't true. What does it take to get through to you? I'm not with you or any other man, is that clear? And don't you ever, and I mean ever, pull this macho nonsense with me again."

She stalked off the floor, leaving behind two hundred and ten pounds of stunned male staring after her.

At the pool tables, she watched Lisa give Doug a good run for his money. He won, but barely, and took a lot of friendly ribbing from the guys over it. Dawn, however, directed her jibes at her sister.

"So this is what you left home for—to shoot pool and hang out with no-account men!"

Lisa grinned and put her arm around Doug's waist. "Hey, they aren't all no-account. Doug here counts real well. Show her honey, show Dawn how you can count." She held up her fingers and Doug obediently counted them.

Dawn laughed and pushed Doug's hat over his eyes. "Now if you can only teach him to read, you can take him home and show him off." They all laughed.

Lisa glanced past Dawn and murmured, "Speaking of show-offs, look who just came in."

A familiar figure, dressed in jeans, boots, and red knit shirt, sat down and hooked his heels on the rung of his barstool, then leaned back with both elbows on the bar behind him. He looked straight at her, smiled a charming smile, and gave her a small salute. Dawn closed her eyes and groaned.

Chapter Nine

"Boy, does he look yummy," Lisa growled.

"Lisa!" Dawn protested, even though she agreed. Matt's posture was aggressively, arrogantly, go-to-blazes male. His hair, as usual, tumbled over his forehead, and for the first time, Dawn realized it was longer than she'd ever seen it.

"Dawn," Lisa warned, "you're staring."

Cheeks blazing, she whipped around, her back to Matt. Behind her, she heard his throaty chuckle.

Doug tried again to teach her the fine points of shooting pool, but too aware of Matt's presence, she couldn't concentrate. When she mis-hit one ball badly enough to send it hopping off the table, she gave up and retreated to where Billy and some of the others sat near the dance floor. She stumbled on her chair leg as she sat down, and was mortified at her clumsiness.

Jerry returned Mary Sills to the table then politely asked Dawn to dance with him. She accepted. Anything to get her mind off Matt.

"Well now, have you cooled off?"

"I beg your pardon?" She raised her chin.

"You're right, I took you for granted and I'm sorry about that. But you called me on it and I took my medicine, so is all forgiven?"

"You misunderstood me, Jerry. We don't have a relationship for you to take for granted. *That* is what I tried to clarify."

"You're still peeved at me."

Dawn sighed. "No Jerry," she explained with exaggerated patience, "I'm not really peeved at you, yet. But I'm getting there."

"Now look here, Dawn, I'm trying to be understanding," he growled, a scowl darkening his features. "I said I was sorry, and I don't do that often. What more do you want?"

They'd stopped dancing and Dawn stood facing him, her hands on her hips. "I guess what I want, Jerry, is distance— as in, between us. You stay on that side of the room and I'll stay on this side of the room." With that, she again left him standing and claimed a chair between two of the men in their group.

Clearly angered now and embarrassed, Jerry started after her but before he reached the table, Matt bent over her shoulder and asked for a dance.

Dawn agreed only as a way to avoid the advancing Jerry, missing completely the irony of having danced with Jerry to avoid thoughts of Matt.

"I couldn't help overhearing," Matt stated in that pleasant voice she'd come to detest. "Distance, huh? Is that the same as freedom?" He pulled her smoothly into his arms and they began circling the floor.

"Yes," she replied succinctly, "it is."

"So good ol' Jerry's struck out, too?"

"What's so hard to understand?" she asked plaintively. "I don't want a relationship; I don't want to belong to anyone. I thought that's what you men liked—no strings, no obligations."

Matt lowered his lips to her ear, his voice a husky whisper. "That's for boys, Dawn. When a man finds the woman he wants, then he wants it all. The obligations, the responsibility, and the respectability. He wants to be there for her, and to be the only one for her. That's what love and marriage are all about."

"Is it?" she bit out sarcastically, but his words sent chills down her spine and tremors through her heart.

"You're a smart woman, Dawn, I'd think you would know all about it," he replied pleasantly.

"Well, I don't," she snapped, "not that version of it."

"Is there another version?"

Dawn didn't answer and Matt let the subject drop. When he returned her to her table, Bev Willis smiled up at them and chided, "Dawn, aren't you going to introduce your friend? Maybe he'd like to join us?"

Dawn shot Matt a look of annoyance, which he met with the warmest, most charming smile she could ever remember seeing. *Oh, brother!* "Matt, this is Bev, Billy, John, Jerry you've met, and over there is Mark, Sarah, Mike, and Leeann. Gang, this is Matt Ivans, my boss."

Bev seemed to be on the verge of drooling, and Dawn heard Sarah mutter under her breath, "I wish my boss looked like that."

Matt took it all in stride, shaking hands with the men and nodding to the women. He greeted Jerry last. With his hands slipped into his back pockets, he nodded to the younger man with a terse, "How's it going?" Jerry nodded back without answering.

Bev eased from her chair in a slow gliding motion and tilted Matt a glance from under partially lowered lashes. "In the interest of neighborliness, let me be the first to welcome you to our little group," she cooed as she took his hand and led him to the dance floor.

"Looks like Mr. Ivans is having a good time," Lisa observed a short while later.

"Doesn't it though." Inexplicably annoyed by the fact, Dawn's irritation increased steadily as the other women all claimed dances, which Matt granted with smiling deference. She finally made a concerted effort not to look at the dance floor at all, which on top of avoiding Jerry's glares, made her feel as though she were threading her way through a mine field.

When Dawn did happen to glance toward the dancers some

time later, Bev had both arms locked around Matt's neck. Matt looked up and Dawn knew he'd caught her furious glare. A fist squeezed her heart at the mocking smile that flitted across his lips and she swung around again, her back to him.

Doug held out his pool cue. "Here, Dawn, let Lisa beat you while I get another round of drinks." When he returned a few minutes later, Matt was at his side, carrying a beer in each hand.

"Working up a thirst there, Tex?" Matt teased. Grinning, he offered her a long-neck.

She accepted the dripping bottle with an arched brow and tilted chin. "Not nearly as much as you are, I'm sure."

Matt's grin grew wider before he lifted the brew to his lips for a long drink. Dawn watched as his lashes drifted closed and his throat worked in swallowing motions. Matt lowered the bottle slowly and wiped the moisture from his lips with a lingering swipe of his thumb. The deliberate gesture strained her breathing. Attempting to hide her reaction, she sipped her own drink, but the amusement in Matt's eyes made her doubt her success.

Doug challenged Matt to a game, and the women stood back to watch. Lisa cheered Doug on; Dawn observed in stony silence. Leaning her hips against the railing, Dawn crossed her arms at her waist and watched the shift and play of muscle as Matt stretched and bent, reached and straightened, stroking shot after shot.

She fought the urge to reach out and touch him. She prayed that the expression on her face hid her inner turmoil, but had her doubts when Matt glanced up and winked.

He laughed when he lost the game by inadvertently sinking the cue ball, then turned to her with a gentle smile. "I'm ready to call it a night. How about giving me one more dance before I turn into a pumpkin?"

She hesitated. He'd dropped the infuriatingly sugary tone and replaced the obnoxious grin with a softly entreating smile that made her heart do a little skip-jump. The confounded man was a chameleon!

"Please?" He held a hand out to her, palm up.

She bit her lip as her gaze dropped to the broad hand. She felt her pulse quicken and her eyes darted back to his. If he noticed, he gave no sign. His eyes reflected only—what? Tenderness?

As though it belonged to someone else, her right hand floated up and came to rest in his outstretched palm. Matt led her down the three steps and through the tables to the parquet floor, then pulled her gently into his arms. Slowly they swayed to the music, oblivious to the other couples moving around them.

Dawn refused to meet his eyes, focusing instead on the tanned wedge of flesh at the base of his corded neck, on the springy wisps of hair that her fingers itched to explore. His Adam's apple slid up and down as he swallowed, and she felt the warmth of his hand as he pulled her closer.

Dawn rested her head against his shoulder, and Matt gave in to the desire to lose himself in the fragrant silkiness of her hair. He laid his cheek on the top of her head just before the end of the first song and inhaled. He'd tipped the disc jockey to play three slow songs in a row with no break between. If he worked this right, that would give him enough time. One song to relax her, one to move in closer, and one to leave her missing him.

Mighty sure of yourself, aren't you? he thought with grim humor. *No, not at all*, came the answer, *but she admitted that she wants me, too, and I plan to use that to my advantage.*

He slowly lifted Dawn's hands and placed them around the back of his neck. She didn't seem to notice the change of songs. He wrapped his arms around her waist and she snuggled her head more comfortably against his shoulder. He felt her sigh.

He kissed her forehead and wished he could be as relaxed as she seemed to be, but in truth, he expected her to come up spitting fire at any moment.

Content to move across the dance floor in his embrace, Dawn recognized this Matt as the man she'd become very fond of. *The man you love.*

Stop that!

She folded her arms tighter. Mesmerized by the music and his nearness, she forgot their current feud as his warm hands held her gently. In her single state, this was what she missed most, simply being held in a man's arms.

Moist breath feathered her hair as his lips brushed her forehead. How heavenly it would be to go on like this forever. No fighting, no pain, no problems, just the music and Matt's arms. And lips. They'd found hers in that moment and were caressing gently.

Nothing intense, the kiss was just a sweet meeting and greeting. Why, then, was her heart racing? *Because you want him to be yours.*

Granted, but so what?

And you love him.

I can't.

It's too late for can't. You already do.

The music stopped and Matt gently pulled her arms from his neck as he whispered, "I have to go now, Dawn." He grazed her lower lip with the pad of this thumb. "Sweet dreams, honey." He lowered his lips to hers and gave her a kiss guaranteed to keep her thinking of him half the night.

Dawn awoke from a delicious dream and groaned. What in the dickens was Matt doing, trying to drive her crazy? His behavior since she'd rejected his declaration of love certainly bore out that theory—or gave evidence to his own shaky hold on reality. At any rate, his regression to world-class grump followed closely by his shift to excessive politeness didn't surprise her nearly as much as the performance he'd put on last night.

He'd managed to ingratiate himself with the group, even though several of the men had initially been jealous of the attention the women gave him. He was gracious in defeat at the pool tables—Dawn suspected his losses were intentional—and his smooth charm when parrying even the most determined female advances won the approval of men and women alike in the end. By the time he'd left, Jerry seemed to be the only one glad to see him go.

And that included herself, Dawn admitted. By the time he'd dipped his head to kiss her good night, she'd been putty in his hands. After that kiss, she more closely resembled a puddle.

That's me, a puddle of Silly Putty. Nearly 3:00 before she'd fallen asleep, and awake again by 4:30 to think of him some more!

Certain Matt's appearance at Fast Freddie's was no coincidence, she still couldn't figure out his motive. *Besides getting revenge by driving me nuts!*

She flopped over on her stomach and pulled the pillow over her head, as if that would block dreams of silver eyes and wicked smiles.

Matt pounded his pillow then flopped his head back down on it. He didn't know whether his campaign to keep himself on Dawn's mind was having any effect on her, but it sure as heck affected him! And that good-night kiss didn't help matters at all.

Staring at the ceiling in the dark, he laced his fingers together on his chest and heaved a sigh. *Way to go, Ivans,* he congratulated himself. *You finally find a woman you want enough to go after and she not only says no, but heck no. And she's a working woman to boot.*

Of course she's a working woman! She's too old to be living at home with Mom and Dad.

But she'd probably be working anyway. She said she likes her freedom.

Yes, but freedom from what? She doesn't seem to have a very high opinion of marriage, maybe that's your clue?

Like maybe she's already tried it and didn't like it?

Exactly. Lisa said Dawn's been through a lot, remember?

I remember.

Matt rolled to his side and tucked the pillow more comfortably under his head. On Monday he'd see what he could find out. He drifted off to sleep with the bed's other pillow clutched in his arms and the remembered scent of Dawn's hair in his nostrils.

"Good morning, Dawn," Matt greeted cheerfully.

Dawn raised her eyebrows, evidently in question at his use of her given name when, in the office, she'd been Ms. Miller for the past two weeks.

He grinned mischievously. "Am I moving too fast? Is it too soon to use your first name?"

She gave her head a quick shake. "What are you babbling about?"

He chuckled. "I thought if we started over from the beginning, maybe we could come up with a different ending. What do you think?" He held his empty coffee cup out to her.

Snatching the cup from his hand, she stalked off to the break room, tossing back over her shoulder, "I think you're insane!"

"Undoubtedly," Matt muttered to himself as he watched her go. "At any rate, I'm crazy about you."

He glanced down at the sheet of statistics laying on his desk. Name, Dawn Louise Miller. Height, five feet, four inches. Age, twenty-four. Marital status, divorced. Not as old as he'd guessed, she'd either been married only a short while, or she'd gotten married awfully young.

Whichever, her youthful bubble had burst leaving her with no desire to repeat the experience. He frowned at the thought of the unknown man who'd left her so emotionally scarred, who'd put that vulnerability in her eyes. Her eyes, deepest brown, fringed with dark honey lashes, wide . . . wary. His hands curled into fists where they rested on his desk.

The telephone at his elbow shrilled. He slid the paper containing Dawn's personal data into a desk drawer and turned his mind to his job. When she returned with his coffee, he gave her a grateful smile as he continued talking on the phone.

"Dawn?" he called a few minutes later.

She swung her head in his direction.

"I'd like you to have lunch with me."

"Mr. Ivans, I don't think that's a good idea."

"We really are starting over, aren't we?" He sighed. "It's an excellent idea, trust me, and please call me Matt."

A smile tugged at one corner of her mouth and he saw it. "It's purely business," he lied. "It's time for your first review."

"I haven't been here three months."

"No, that would be your second review, your first is at six weeks."

Dawn's brows drew into a delicate frown. She didn't want to call Matt a liar, and for the life of her she couldn't remember the interviewer saying when her first evaluation would be. "All right," she said slowly.

"Good. If you don't mind, we'll wait until one o'clock to go. The restaurant won't be as busy then."

Dawn did her best to sound neutral, hiding her doubts. "No, one is fine."

At the little Mexican restaurant, Maria showed them to a secluded corner booth, treating Matt far more warmly than she had during their last meal here. They placed their orders and she immediately returned with their drinks.

Moving his cola aside, Matt took a leather-bound portfolio from his briefcase, flipped it open, and scanned its contents. He took a pen from his pocket and sat back, clearly prepared to make notes.

"So, Dawn, how do you like working for StarAmerica so far? Any complaints?"

She eyed him suspiciously. "Matt, what are you up to?"

"I've already told you, we're playing boss and subordinate. Now listen up." Writing on the pad he muttered to himself, "No complaints."

"I didn't say that."

"Oh. Well, do you have any complaints?"

"Not for the official record."

Matt grinned. "Like I said, no complaints. Do you feel your pay is fair for the job you do?"

"Yes, until I get better at it."

He nodded and made another note.

"Do you feel the office atmosphere is favorable for your best work effort?"

This had to be the strangest review Dawn had ever heard

of. "Yes, for the most part. Matt, this sounds more like a survey than an evaluation."

"Well, it's both," he explained blithely. "You're evaluating the job, and I'm evaluating you. Now for you. It says here you're only twenty-four. I would have guessed you a little older."

"Thank you, I think."

Matt smiled and nodded, not taking his eyes from the doodles on the page in front of him. "It was intended as a compliment. Let's see, business school education, placed high in your class, very good." Then he lifted his eyes to hers, his expression schooled to one of mild interest. "You're divorced?"

"Yes." Alarm flared in Dawn's eyes, bringing back the haunted look.

He clenched his jaw, wishing for five minutes with her ex-husband, then took a sip of his iced drink to give his voice time to modulate before he continued innocently, "And how long ago was that?"

"Almost two y . . ." Her voice cracked. She cleared her throat. "Two years."

"Did you work while you were married?" he asked without looking up.

"No, Mr. Ivans," Dawn said formally, "I didn't, and I fail to see what that has to do with anything. If you don't mind my saying so, most of those questions seem a little odd."

Matt tipped his head to one side and studied the woman across from him. "I suppose they do. Does it bother you to talk about your divorce?"

"Yes, it does."

"Why? It's nothing unusual anymore. You don't have to be embarrassed about it."

"It may not be unusual, but that doesn't mean it isn't painful."

"Is it for you?"

Dawn lifted wide troubled eyes to his, "What?"

"Is talking about your divorce painful for you?"

"Yes." She dropped her gaze again.

"I'm sorry, I'd hoped to get to know you better. Maybe someday you'll feel comfortable enough with me to discuss it."

Already well beyond the bounds of company policy and labor laws, Matt knew he was pressing his luck. If anyone found out about this "interview," he'd lose his job. He'd have to drop the charade for now.

"What about you?"

He looked up from tucking the portfolio back into his briefcase. "What about me?"

"Are you divorced?"

"Nope. Never lucky enough to find a woman who'd have me."

Dawn chuckled remembering the impact he'd had on the women at the pool hall. The impact he had on her. "Then you must have been looking in a convent."

Matt grinned. "Okay, so maybe I never found one I wanted to pledge my life to before."

Before. Would he offer to do that for her? He'd said he loved her. "Matt, why are we here, really?"

They were interrupted by the arrival of their meal. Maria hovered over them solicitously until they'd both tasted of their food and assured her it was perfect, then she ambled off, humming.

"Matt." Dawn wanted an answer.

He shrugged and gave her a guilty little smile. "I told you. I want to get to know you better."

"Then don't play games with me. If you have a question, ask it. If I want you to know, I'll answer it."

He folded his hands together, index fingers against his lips as he leaned his elbows on the table. His gray eyes were steady and solemn as they met hers across the table. "That's the problem, I don't think you want me to know."

"Because it's none of your business," she answered quietly.

"But I want to make it my business, Dawn." He reached for her hand and covered it with his own. "I want to make *you* my business. You know that, don't you?"

She nodded and whispered, "I know."

"I'm not asking out of idle curiosity. I want to know why you're shutting me out."

She snatched her hand back. "Is it a new experience for you or something?"

"Yes! No! You know what I mean."

She watched him bluster in the face of her taunt. "I'm not sure I do, Matt. What exactly do you mean?"

She watched him grit his teeth in an obvious attempt to control his temper, then he leaned forward and growled, "What I mean is, you've admitted you feel something for me, but you won't give it a chance and I want to know why."

"Oh, that."

"Yes, that!"

"I've already told you," Dawn explained patiently, "I don't want another relationship. I'm happy taking care of myself."

"But you haven't explained why, Dawn. You haven't told me why you think you'd be happier alone than with a man who loves you."

Matt's hands were braced against the edge of the table. His jaw, set in tense lines, bulged as he worked his teeth together. His eyes flashed like sparks off polished steel. Heavens, but he was magnificent.

She fought the urge to push his hair back from his forehead and trail her fingertips over the clenched muscles of his face until they lost that hard, angry edge. As she watched, his expression transformed. His jet brows relaxed from their puckered scowl to curve over his silver eyes, and the muscles in his jaw smoothed out.

He dropped his head, as though in defeat, and muttered, "Dawn, don't look at me like that. Not if you won't let me do anything about it."

"Like what? What are you talking about?"

"When you aren't snapping at me, you have the look of a wounded animal. Your eyes beg me to take you in and make everything all right."

"You're crazy!"

"Right, whatever." He sighed wearily. "Are you finished eating?"

She hesitated, studying his features, his defeated expression, before murmuring, "I'll tell you about it."

"What?"

"I'll tell you about my divorce, but not now. It will have to be after work sometime."

"How about tonight? We could go somewhere quiet for dinner."

"Okay." She sighed. "But don't expect it to change anything."

They drove to the same steakhouse he'd taken her to for their first date. On a Monday evening the place was nearly deserted and a corner table afforded them relative privacy. When their dinner orders were placed, Dawn leaned back in her chair and toyed with the stem of her water glass while she gathered courage to begin.

"Ready?" she finally asked.

He nodded.

"Okay, here goes." She decided to begin at the beginning, and tell him everything. "When I was barely nineteen I found myself pregnant. Dave and I had been dating all through high school, so we just moved our wedding up a couple of years. For a while everything was perfect. He'd been working for a building contractor for almost a year and made decent money." She paused for a sip of water, then continued. "About four months after our wedding, the economy took a nosedive and building fell way off. Dave had to go out of town more and more for work.

"He'd come home when he had a weekend off and between jobs, but I didn't see him much during that time." She paused in remembrance, her eyes threatening to tear.

"He was there when our daughter was born, but the rest of the year turned out to be more of the same. He'd be home four days a month at the most. Taking care of the baby kept me busy."

The memories pulled at her, tugging down the corners of her mouth, curling her brows together in a frown. She wouldn't be able to tell Matt everything after all, she realized. She couldn't bear to hear it herself.

Drawing a shuddering breath she cut the story short, finishing with a shrug. "Then one day I got a letter from him with divorce papers enclosed. He'd found someone new and wanted to marry her."

"Son of a . . ." Matt rasped in a low whisper.

She smiled weakly. "Tell me about it."

In hope of forestalling any questions, she hurried on. "So now you know why I don't care to trust my happiness and well-being to anyone but myself. After all, that's really the way it should be. If we all took care of ourselves instead of burdening someone else with that responsibility, the world would be a better place, don't you agree?"

It didn't work. Matt studied her for just a heartbeat before asking quietly, "Where's your daughter?"

She bit her lip. When it began to quiver, she bit harder, trying to stop it. She tasted blood. Tears blurred her vision and she heard Matt suck in his breath. When she looked up, his eyes were as stricken as her own. He reached across the table and grasped both her hands, hard.

"Oh, sweetheart, no," he whispered.

Slowly, she nodded her head. "She's gone, Matt. My sweet little Julie is gone." She choked back a sob.

Chapter Ten

In an instant Matt was around the table and on one knee at her side, pulling her against him. "I'm sorry," he murmured urgently against her hair. "I'm so sorry, honey. Please don't cry. You don't have to tell me anything, I'm sorry."

"There's not much else to tell." Drawing a shaky breath, she fought for control. "She was only fifteen months old when she contracted meningitis. I didn't know she was so sick; at first I thought she had a cold. By the time I got her to the hospital the doctors couldn't do much, it had gone too far."

Another sob choked her and Matt tightened his hold. "Let's get out of here," he murmured. She nodded in agreement and he straightened. "Wait here, I'll be right back."

In a couple of minutes he returned with their dinners packed in Styrofoam containers and held out his hand to her. "Come on."

One arm wrapped securely around her shoulders, he walked her out to the car. When she'd fastened her seat belt, he handed her their dinners, then headed the powerful machine toward town.

"I'm sorry," Dawn whispered.

He reached across the console for her hand and gave it a reassuring squeeze. "Shhh. You don't have anything to apologize for."

Fingers interlaced, their hands rested on the console between them and she drew comfort from the sight of her smaller hand nestled in the warmth of his wide strong palm.

Matt exited the highway in an area unfamiliar to her. A neighborhood of neat little houses behind neat little lawns, it gave way to a couple of blocks of modest garden homes. At a stop sign, she saw the next two or three blocks were occupied by two-story townhouses.

"Where are we going?"

"To my place. We still need to eat, but I thought you would appreciate a little privacy."

A moment later Matt unlocked the door and relieved her of the boxes, motioning for her to follow with a jerk of his head. "Come on back to the kitchen and we'll reheat these right quick."

The ceramic-tiled entry cut between a carpeted living room on the right and dining room on the left. She noted the front room was decorated in a modified Southwest style, light colors with masculine-sized furniture. A shield of sorts, made of leather stretched over a round frame and trimmed with beads, bits of fur, and bright feathers hung over the sofa. Small shelves mounted on the wall held Native American pottery.

A pickled wood table with matching chairs held center stage in the formal dining room. Flame-stitched upholstery in pale turquoise and peach covered the chair cushions and framed watercolors of Indian villages in complementing colors adorned the walls. In the center of the table, a handsome terra-cotta bowl held an arrangement of silk flowers.

Dawn discovered more pickled wood in the kitchen and white tile countertops. The appliances were a sand beige. The room was surprisingly neat, except for the breakfast bar. A jumble of mail and newspapers littered its top, along with a pair of pliers, a mug with a broken handle, and a large bottle of aspirin.

All in all, Matt's place was more attractive and much neater than she'd expected a bachelor's pad would be, but she'd never seen another, so she had no real frame of reference.

He opened a cabinet and began withdrawing dinnerware.

"Can I help?" she offered.

"Sure, if you don't mind setting the table. Take these in

and I'll bring our plates." He handed her silverware, glasses, napkins, and placemats.

While she set the table he transferred the food onto the dinnerware for reheating. The plates took turns in the microwave oven as he opened a bottle of wine and carried it to the table. A few minutes later they sat facing each other and Dawn suddenly felt self-conscious.

"Now, isn't this better? We can continue any discussion we might want without worrying what strangers are thinking about us." Matt grinned disarmingly before popping a chunk of steak into his mouth.

"I think I'm pretty well talked out," she murmured, dropping her attention to her plate.

"I can understand that." He sat back in his chair and took a sip of wine. "I had no idea it was such a Pandora's box."

She cast him a speculative look. "But you aren't sorry you opened it."

"No," he agreed slowly. "I needed to know what I'm up against."

"Well, now you know."

"Yes, now I know. When you've eaten would you mind telling me what came next?"

She hesitated, at a loss for words.

"I'd really be interested in hearing how you went from being a teenaged housewife to a liberated woman," he cajoled.

Was he teasing her? Making fun of her? She couldn't detect it in his voice or expression. He sat there, his silver eyes leveled on her in an open, honest gaze.

Why not? She might as well get it over with all at once.

"Okay, but I may have some questions for you, too."

He chuckled. "Fair enough. More wine?"

In the living room, Dawn slipped off her shoes and curled in one corner of the sofa with her bare feet tucked under her. Matt had shed his jacket and tie and opened the top two buttons on his shirt. He refilled their wineglasses and handed her one, then sat on the other half of the couch, his body angled toward her.

"So," he began, "what did you do when you received the 'Dear Joan' letter with divorce papers enclosed?"

"It was after Julie'd died and I lost what little sanity I'd been clinging to," she replied flatly as she stared into her wine.

"I'll bet."

"She'd only been gone a few months. I'd taken a job to keep up with the bills, and to try to keep my mind busy, but even after putting in a full day at the grocery store, I'd be in the shower and think I heard her cry. More than once I'd be halfway out of the tub before I remembered it couldn't be her."

She paused to take a steadying sip of her drink and Matt reached over to give her shoulder a comforting squeeze. The tender gesture was reassuring. She forged on.

"When Dave's letter came and I realized that the home I'd tried so hard to maintain for us didn't exist, that it was over, all of it, I just sort of shut down. Like my mind couldn't take any more. I guess it could best be described as a walking coma. I pretty much functioned on automatic for several months, getting up, going to work, going home to eat and sleep—not that I did much of either—then doing it all over again."

"What about your family?"

"They tried to help, but if I got outside my mindless routine, I'd start thinking again, remembering, and I just couldn't handle it."

She drew a deep breath and let it out in a shaky sigh. "If I didn't think, I didn't feel, and if I didn't feel, I could make it one more day."

Matt set his glass on the coffee table and moved closer to her, taking her hand and covering it on his bent knee. Idly stroking his thumb up and down the backs of her fingers, he asked, "How long did this go on?"

"About eight months, I guess."

He groaned softly.

"Anyway," she continued, trying to sound more upbeat, "on the anniversary of Julie's death I realized I had to get on with my life. It would not be a credit to her memory if her mommy died in a fit of depression, so I decided to make something of myself in tribute to her instead. I applied for grants and student loans, worked all the hours I could schedule around my classes, and went to business school. The rest, as they say, is history."

Matt pressed her hand against his leg. "Yeah, I guess it is."

She cocked her head and raised an eyebrow at him, a wry smile twisting her mouth. "So you see, Mr. Ivans, why your threat to fire me had little impact."

He frowned in puzzlement for a moment as she took a sip of wine. She watched him over the rim of her glass, as the day of their first really big blow-up crystallized in his memory.

"Oh . . . my . . . God." He gasped.

"Exactly."

His head dropped back against the couch and he closed his eyes as he muttered, "I even managed to say something about staying home with babies, didn't I?"

"You sure did."

"And that's what made you cry." He shook his head. "I always wondered what I'd said. Dawn, I'm so sorry. I didn't know."

"No, you didn't," she agreed levelly.

"I can't believe I did that!"

"Like you said, you had no way of knowing. Besides, it isn't any worse than my crack about being crippled."

"Yes it is, much worse."

"Neither of us said those things to be hurtful, Matt, and now that we know better, I'm sure we won't do it again."

He heaved a great sigh of relief. "You are one incredible woman, do you know that?"

"Darn straight, flyboy." Dawn gave him a saucy smirk.

He threw back his head and laughed, and she smiled in spite of herself, basking in the warmth of his approval. It really would be so easy to love this man. She watched the laughter soften his craggy features, crinkling those arresting silver-blue eyes, the deep masculine sound of his mirth warming the chill around her heart.

Suddenly he fell quiet and the smile faded from his lips.

He lifted a hand and let the backs of his fingers drift lightly down the side of her face. "You are so special."

An accolade straight from his heart. A shiver ran down her spine and she suddenly remembered all the endearments he'd used this evening. He'd reached out to her through her pain with words of love and caring. He'd called her sweetheart.

Abruptly, she dropped her gaze. "I need to be going."

"Don't run off so soon, it's early yet."

"Tomorrow is a workday, and I have to be rested and fortified. I work for Ivans the Terrible, you know." She stood and slipped her feet into her pumps.

Matt rose and stood close. Taking her chin in his hand, he tipped it up to meet his gaze. "Is he really all that terrible, Dawn?"

No, her heart shouted. *He's wonderful. He's warm, and handsome, and caring, and strong. . . .* "He can be when he doesn't get his way."

He smiled, a slow, sexy widening of his lips. "Then why don't you simply let him have his way?"

"It wouldn't be good for his character development."

Surprised, delighted laughter burst from Matt again and he pulled her into his arms, hugging her tightly.

She leaned back when he loosened his embrace and looked up into his sparkling silver eyes. "Matt?"

"Hmmm?"

"Deep down, you're really not an unreasonable person."

A quizzical frown pinched his brows. "Thanks, I think."

"So why do you act like you do at work?"

"How do I act at work?"

She swatted his arm in reprimand. "You know what I mean. That caveman 'woman belongs in the kitchen' bit."

He sighed and released her. Shoving his hands into his pockets, he paced across the room and back again. Dawn waited. He stopped in front of her and brushed her cheek with his thumb.

"It's only fair, I guess," he muttered. "You told me your story, so I suppose you're entitled to hear mine." He motioned to the sofa and Dawn perched on the edge of a cushion. He remained on his feet and resumed his pacing.

"You know I was in the Army."

She nodded.

"You know I crashed my chopper."

"I was told it malfunctioned."

"Whatever."

Matt stalked across the room and turned abruptly to face her.

"There were several serious injuries among my crew."

"I can imagine," Dawn offered.

"No, you can't imagine," he snapped. The dragon was back. "You can't imagine what it's like to be at the controls, the one in charge when all hell breaks loose. Those people were my crew, my responsibility!"

"It wasn't your fault," she insisted.

He spun away from her. "So they say."

"Then why can't you forgive yourself? You were hurt, too!"

"But I lived," he snarled in self-disgust.

"Of course you . . ." She stopped, a sense of foreboding skittering down her spine. "Someone died of their injuries?" she whispered.

"No. Someone died outright. At the moment of impact."

"Oh, Matt. I'm so sorry." She puzzled over his revelation a moment, then said, "I still don't understand what that has to do with—"

"It was a woman! My dead crew chief was a woman!" Matt's face contorted in rage; his eyes burned with unspeakable pain.

Dawn gasped and pressed her fingertips to her lips.

"Sgt. Kathy Smith, U.S. Army, left behind a loving husband and two handsome, smart, preteen sons!"

Matt sank to the couch and shoved his hands through his hair. "She shouldn't have been there," he whispered. "She should have been home with her boys."

Dawn rested a hand between his slumped shoulders. "Matt, would it have been any better for the boys to lose their father?

Losing a parent is tragic; so is losing a spouse. But is it easier for one gender than the other? I don't think so."

She began rubbing soothing circles between his taut muscles. "You are a good man, Matt Ivans. The fact that you grieve so deeply for Kathy proves what a good officer you were, but it's time to let it go. It's time to forgive yourself."

He sighed deeply and looked over at her, a small twisted smile on his lips. "You think so?"

"I know so," she replied softly. "Take it from the voice of experience."

He took her hand and turned it palm up to study the lines. "Yeah, I guess you'd know, huh?" He placed a kiss in her palm before leaning back and closing his eyes. He sighed, then opened them again. "Quite a night."

"Yes, it has been. I'm glad you told me, Matt."

"I'm glad you shared, too."

"I really do need to be leaving, though."

He sat up. "I suppose you're sure about that as well?"

She smiled, as he'd intended. "Yes, I'm sure."

"Okay, you win. I'll save the grand tour of the house for another time."

"I'd like that, Matt . . . another time," she said quietly.

They headed for his car in companionable silence.

"Thank you for telling me everything." Matt reached out and shut off the car's ignition. "I can only imagine how hard that must have been for you."

He draped his wrist on the back of her seat, his hand so close to her cheek Dawn could feel the heat of it. She closed her eyes and whispered, "Hard doesn't begin to touch it."

"I know. I'm sorry."

The backs of his fingers began stroking her skin and Dawn fought the urge to lean into his hand, to clasp it to her face, to absorb his touch. "I'm told it gets easier as time goes by, but no one seems to know how much time."

She looked out the window and attempted to mask the threatening tears behind a shaky smile. "Maybe in a hundred years?"

"Maybe. Or with help it could be sooner. I'd like to help, you know."

"I know, but I think now you understand why I can't let that happen."

"No, but I understand why it may take longer than I expected it to."

"Matt—"

"Come on," he interrupted, "I'll walk you to the door."

He took her hand as they climbed the stairs. At the door he turned her into his arms for a tender kiss. "Good night, sweetheart," he whispered, then opened the door to her apartment and pushed her gently inside.

Much to her surprise, Dawn slept soundly all night. She'd been emotionally exhausted by the time she'd fallen into bed and had expected to be troubled by dreams of David or nightmares of Julie. But there must have been some healing in the telling, in Matt's compassionate reassurance, because her rest had been deep and peaceful.

"How'd it go?" Lisa stood over the sink with a slice of toast and a cup of coffee.

"About as you'd expect. You know how hard it is for me to talk about. But I managed and now that he knows, I'm sure Matt will give up gracefully."

Lisa almost choked on her coffee. "Don't bet on it!"

"Why do you say that?"

"Dawn," her sister drawled in exasperation, "the man is in love with you. I don't think that's happened to him too many times before in his life, if ever, and he's not the kind to give up without a fight."

"Oh Lisa, Matt doesn't really love me. He's interested, is all, and that mostly because I turned him down."

"Yeah, sure."

"Hurry up or we'll be late for work."

Matt greeted her with a warm smile and a pleasant "Good morning". Dawn performed her morning routine and he thanked her for the coffee. All the tension of the past weeks dissolved, leaving Dawn very glad she'd confided in him. They could never become romantically involved, but the thought of not having him in her life at all had thrown her into a panic. Now they were friends again, and she treasured that.

Mid-morning the phone on her desk rang. "Hello? Oh, hi Jerry. . . . Thank you, but I don't think so. . . . I'm sorry, Jerry, but I told you from the beginning I didn't want any entanglements and you just pushed too hard."

Matt listened discreetly to the one-sided conversation.

"We did not 'have something going'. . . . I'm sorry too, but I'm very glad we met. . . . What a sweet thing to say, thank you. . . . Yes, I'm sure I'll see you around. 'Bye."

When Dawn replaced the receiver and glanced up he asked, "Problem?"

"No, not at all."

"Let me know if there is."

"I will." She smiled to herself thinking that would be like asking a cat to help guard the birdcage.

When she left for lunch, Matt asked her to bring him back a cheeseburger. Her mood had mellowed so much that she didn't notice anything unusual when he said, "Thanks, sweetheart," as he accepted the bag from her an hour later. She simply smiled in return and put her purse away.

Lisa heard about it by the afternoon coffee break, but didn't mention it to her sister.

Dawn rolled over and hit her alarm clock, but the ringing continued. Groggily she realized the noise came from the telephone in the next room. She squinted at the lighted numbers on the clock face. 1:10 A.M. Guess who.

With a groan she threw back the covers and stumbled out of bed. Lisa had been known to sleep through a hurricane, so Dawn knew a ringing phone had no chance of waking her.

"H'llo?"

"Dawn?" The voice was raspy and male.

"Yes."

"What are you wearing?"

"What?"

"Something frilly, I bet."

"Who is this? Just leave me alone!"

"White satin or black lace?" the voice continued, ignoring her response.

She slammed the receiver down and took a quick step back as though the telephone could reach out and grab her. Hands shaking, she hurried back to her room and buried herself in her bed.

She had an overwhelming urge to call Matt, but to do that she'd need to leave her safe haven. Instead, she pulled the quilt over her head and tried to go back to sleep. The voice interfered with her slumber for the rest of the night, though, weaving in and out of her dreams. This was the first time he'd used her name.

In the morning, Lisa noticed. "Aren't you feeling well? You look a little frazzled."

"Our caller checked in again last night."

"Oh? Sorry I missed him. Did he come up with anything new?"

"Just my name."

"What?"

"He called me by name."

"No! I don't guess you recognized his voice?"

Remembering it, Dawn shivered. "Of course not. He whispered so I wouldn't."

"Do you think we should call the police?"

"No. It's probably one of the gang, with too much to drink and too much time on his hands."

"On a Tuesday night? I doubt it."

So did Dawn, but she didn't want to think about it anymore.

That afternoon, she returned from lunch to find a small florist's box on her desk. She smiled and glanced in Matt's direction before lifting the lid. The box contained a small cactus plant in a clay pot. A note impaled on the plant read: *I'm totally stuck on you.*

"More flowers?" Matt looked over her shoulder then

growled. "What the . . . who sent you that?" He plucked the small card from her trembling fingers and read it. "Dawn?"

"I . . . I don't know. Last night, a call." A chill washed her skin and set her to shaking.

"What call?" he asked as his warm hand gently stroked her arm. "Tell me."

"Oh, a . . . a prank call, that's all, only a prank," she stammered. "Just someone's idea of a joke."

"It's not very funny."

"No," she agreed, "it isn't."

"Is it the same guy? Have you notified the police?"

"Of course not. It's just some nut getting his kicks. I hung up on him. That's what the experts say to do, isn't it? Don't give these guys an audience and they move on to someone who will?"

Matt gestured to the box. "What about this?"

She shrugged.

Matt poked the flowerpot and frowned. "Let me know if you get any more calls or gifts.' "

"I'm sure I won't."

"Dawn."

"Okay, I promise. Thanks, Matt."

Chapter Eleven

When the telephone rang that evening, Dawn jumped. Lisa leaned over the back of the couch and picked up the receiver.

"Hello? Oh, hi Mr. Ivans. Yes, she's here, just a minute."

Lisa grinned and waggled the phone in the air. "Dawn, there's a Mr. Ivans on the line, will you accept the call?"

Dawn made a face at her sister and reached for the receiver, but Lisa jerked it back out of her reach. "One moment please, Mr. Ivans, and she'll be right with you," Lisa crooned before relinquishing the instrument.

Dropping into a corner of the sofa, Dawn propped her feet up. "Hello, Matt."

"Good evening. I think you have more than one telephone prankster around there."

"I'm afraid so." She sighed.

"At least that one's harmless."

"The other one is too, just more unnerving."

"Hmmm, I hope you're right."

"No offense, Matt, but did you call just to stir up unpleasant memories, or do you have some other reason?"

"Since you ask, I called just to hear the musical tones of your voice."

"Oh brother, another prank call."

"I'm hurt!"

"Sure you are." She scooted down more comfortably on the sofa, a smile playing at her lips.

"Am I interrupting something or do you have time to chat?"

"No, we were trying to decide whether to fry our brains watching television, or write letters to our folks."

"Tell Lisa to say hi for you in her letter—then you'll be free to talk to me."

"Matt, what's up?"

"Nothing." His tone became serious. "I wanted to be sure you're all right."

"I'm fine, why wouldn't I be?" Dawn settled into a more comfortable position on the sofa and pulled a pillow into her lap. "Are you sure that's all?"

"That, and I really did want to hear your voice."

As before, his warm honeyed tone sent little bubbles racing along her bloodstream, and she gave a nervous laugh. "You hear it all day long, isn't that enough?"

"That's just it. I've gotten used to hearing you in the background throughout the day, so when I come home at night to my empty house it's even lonelier without you."

Why was he doing this to her? If it weren't for his tone, Dawn would swear Matt was still teasing, but the deep timbre left no doubt as to his sincerity. His concern warmed her, but the longing in his last words sent a tingle up her spine. Was that possible, being warmed and chilled at the same time?

"Dawn?" His voice pulled her from her confused contemplation of the way he affected her.

"I'm here."

"I wish you were here instead."

"Matt," she pleaded. The vibrations of his low growl were playing havoc with her nervous system and pulse rate.

"Still not ready to give in, huh?" He gave an exaggerated sigh. "You will, you know. Someday you'll see all the fun you're missing by keeping me at a distance. Deep down I'm really a terrific guy, nothing at all like the one that shows up at the office."

She couldn't help but laugh. "I'll bet you're modest, too."

"Yep. And brave, and loyal, and trustworthy."

"A real scout."

"Nope, I never was much of a tracker, unless you're talking about the tire marks left by a four-wheel-drive truck in soft mud."

She laughed again. How many years had it been since she'd talked nonsense on the telephone with a member of the opposite sex? It seemed like an eternity. "That's okay, I always carry a map and a compass in my car."

"See? We'd make a great team. In fact, we already do. Did you see today's reports? We're in the number-one slot for productivity again, and we're a good ten percent ahead of number two."

"Really? That's great, congratulations."

"Couldn't do it without you, sweetheart."

"You did it before I came," she reminded him, ignoring the endearment.

"But not by this big a margin. We have to celebrate. How about dinner Friday night?"

"Matt . . ."

"Oh, come on, Miller, loosen up. You're becoming an old fuddy-duddy."

"A what?" she sputtered.

"It's one of my mother's expressions. It means a fussy, grumpy . . ."

"I know what it means." Dawn gasped between spasms of laughter. "It just sounds hilarious coming from you."

Matt snorted.

"I'll bet"—she paused to laugh again—"I'll bet you never called one of your soldiers that."

Matt chuckled at the idea. "No, you're right about that. So, back to the subject—dinner Friday."

"Oh, all right."

"Gracious in defeat as always," he teased.

She fell silent for a moment. She really did feel much better after talking with him. "Matt, thank you for calling."

"My pleasure." He'd dropped the bantering tone and his voice brushed over her skin like warmed velvet. "Good night, sweetheart, I'll see you in the morning."

* * *

Dawn slept like a log. She'd half expected visions of cacti and the echoes of a raspy voice to disturb her rest but they never materialized. Just as before, when she'd shared her painful past with Matt, she awoke rested and refreshed.

That ought to tell you something.

Hush.

Humming to herself, she scanned her closet. The flowered dress she'd bought just before Easter caught her eye and she smiled. Why not? Matt liked it and said she could wear it to work, and with a white linen jacket it wouldn't be too inappropriate. She might even leave her hair down.

When she reached work, the security guard at the bank door greeted her with a wide smile. "My, my, don't you look fine as a spring mornin' today."

She grinned at the aging man. "Thank you, Mr. Wade, I feel as fine, too."

When Matt saw her, he gave a long, low whistle of appreciation. "Well, just look at you. Could I interest you in an early lunch, say at the café by the Holiday Inn? Then we could just get a room, and—"

"Matthew Ivans, behave yourself before someone hears you! You're going to get yourself fired with nonsense like that."

He gave her a bemused grin. "Nonsense?" he repeated.

"You never know who's listening," she reminded him in exasperation, "and they might not realize you're teasing. And even if they did, I've told you it's inappropriate. Lawsuits have been filed for less cause."

"Doggone it, Dawn, it's *not* inappropriate," he hissed, his voice a harsh whisper. "I've told you I love you. I'm not some lecher trying to seduce his secretary; I want to *marry* you. There's a difference, you know!"

What? "Marry me?"

"Of course." He sighed. "What did you think I had in mind? You know I love you, and I've told you before what that means in my book. Commitment, responsibility, the works."

He stood and took her by the shoulders, his eyes soft and shining. "This isn't what I'd planned, not here, not like this, but how about it? Would you please put me out of my misery by marrying me?"

"Matt I . . . I can't." Her eyes quickly filled with tears. "I'm sorry, but I just can't. Please understand."

Hurt wiped the joy from his face, but Matt clamped down on it. Dawn wasn't ready yet and he knew it, but biding his time came hard. He'd waited all his life for this woman to come along, and now impatience dogged his every waking hour.

"You can," he told her, softly encouraging, "and you will. I'll wait, sweetheart. Never fear, I'll wait."

His telephone rang, bringing them both back to an awareness of their surroundings. He turned reluctantly to his desk and Dawn pulled out her chair.

Dawn's phone rang a moment later. She took a deep breath, shifting gears emotionally, and picked it up.

"Hello, this is Dawn."

"It sure is," the whispered voice agreed. "It's the dawn of a new day, honey. Did you wear that dress just for me?"

"Who is this?" she demanded. He knew what she was wearing! "Leave me alone! Just leave me alone!"

"You sorry son of an egg-sucking dog, stay away from her!" Matt's voice thundered in her ear.

Matt had switched over to Dawn's line when he heard her demanding to be left alone. The caller laughed. "Yeah, right. You'll be hearing from me, honey," he promised Dawn, then hung up.

Matt slammed his phone down then turned to take her receiver from her shaking fingers. She was trembling too badly to even put it back in its cradle. Reaching across her desk, he dropped it in place then knelt beside her chair. "It's the same guy, isn't it?"

Dawn nodded.

"Are you okay?" He grasped her hands, and found they were like ice. "Can I get you something?"

She shook her head. "Just stay with me for a minute," she whispered. "Don't leave me."

"Never." He gave her fingers a reassuring squeeze. "I'm right here, sweetheart, for as long as you want."

His ringing telephone went unanswered and when Dawn's phone rang again he snatched up the receiver and barked, "Ivans."

His supervisor asked, "You're not answering your line, and I heard you yelling. Is everything all right over there?"

"Sorry, Bill. Not really. I need to talk to you and to our head of security."

"Security? Do you need a guard?"

"No, nothing like that, we aren't being hijacked. But I do need to talk to security."

"You've got it. When?"

"Just a minute." Matt muffled the mouthpiece on his leg and looked at Dawn. "Are you up to reporting on this yet?"

She shook her head vehemently.

"Dawn, this isn't just a random crank—he knows who you are. He has your home number and he knows where you work. You need to report this." He could feel her trembling start anew.

"Would . . . would you do it for me? You know as much about it as I do. Except . . ."

"Except what, honey?"

Her eyes widened in terror. "Don't call me that!"

"I'm sorry, he called you that, didn't he? What were you going to tell me?"

"I think he . . . he's watching me. He knows what I'm wearing today."

Matt muttered a vile curse. He didn't like the implications of Dawn's statement.

"Will you?" Dawn pleaded.

"Of course. But they might want to talk to you later, you know."

"I know," she replied softly. "I just can't right now."

He placed a kiss on her forehead and stood. "I don't blame you. Can I go yet, or do you want me to wait a while?"

"Go ahead."

"Are you sure?"

She nodded. "I'll be okay, now. Thanks."

"Anytime, sweetheart, you know that. I'll be back as soon as I can." He uncovered the phone. "I'm coming over now, Bill."

Shortly after Matt left, Lilly appeared and, uninvited, propped a hip on the corner of Matt's desk and began regaling Dawn with the details of her wild weekend at the lake. It took Dawn only a couple of minutes to realize that Matt had sent the girl as a diversion. Even in his absence, he looked out for her.

Matt paced in front of Bill's desk, waiting for the bank's security supervisor. Bill eyed him shrewdly.

"Why so uptight, Matt? Everyday thousands of women across America get unwanted phone calls. Not a pleasant fact, but it's sure nothing new."

"That doesn't mean I have to sit still for it," Matt snarled.

Bill sat back in his chair, his elbows braced on the arms, and folded his hands together, resting his index fingers against his lips. Matt's superior studied him thoughtfully for several moments before speaking again.

"Can I assume that this one's worked out all right?"

"What?"

"Your clerk—"

"Dawn," Matt interrupted.

"Dawn," Bill acknowledged. "You've developed a good working relationship with her?"

"Not really."

"Oh." Bill decided he'd misread the situation. "You don't want to continue with her as your clerk?"

"No, I don't," Matt growled. "I want to continue with her as my wife."

"Your what?"

"You heard me."

A wide grin split Bill's weathered face and he rose to offer Matt his hand. "Congratulations, it's about time!"

"Thanks, but she won't have me. Yet."

Matt related what he knew about Dawn's first calls, the cactus, and what he'd overheard that day. Looking at the security man, he finished, "I think it's someone in this building."

"What makes you say that?"

"He knew what she had on today."

The man nodded his close-cropped head as he made some notes. "You have a point there," he agreed. "The guy knows how to reach her at home, so he knows her last name, too."

The bank's head of security had the look of an overaged prize fighter. Crooked nose, large body gone slightly soft, wide beefy hands, but he possessed a keen intelligence undimmed by any blows to the head. Buck Adams was, in fact, a former intelligence officer in the United States military.

"I suppose he does, but it's worse than that," Matt supplied. "Dawn is sharing her sister's apartment, the telephone is in Lisa's name, and they have different last names. Dawn's been married."

Buck frowned at this new bit of information. "The ex-husband or a friend of the sister's, maybe?"

Matt shrugged. "Could be, but I doubt it. He's remarried. Besides, Lisa works here too, in Accounts Receivable."

Buck grunted and jotted that down on his notepad, then looked up at Matt. "I think we'd better notify the cops."

An officer took the report over the phone and informed Dawn that unless her agitator actually made a move against her, they couldn't do much. He suggested she simply call the telephone company and have her number changed. She hung up, discouraged.

"Don't worry," Buck said and made a note of the time of her call and the name of the officer she'd spoken with. "That's just what I expected. Now call the phone company."

She did and found them a little more supportive. They would change Lisa's number to an unlisted one for a limited period of time, or they would change it permanently.

Buck got on the line and identified himself. "We would like a tap and a tracer on the line," he requested. "What sort of documentation do you need?"

The bank changed Dawn's work extension and calls to her

old number would route through Matt's phone. "Great," she muttered, "now he'll just go back to calling me at home in the middle of the night."

"When it's dark and you're all alone?" Matt teased.

"It's not funny!"

"I know it isn't, sweetheart, but I don't plan to leave you out there alone. I'm going to camp out on your couch."

"Don't be ridiculous."

"I've already cleared it with Lisa."

"Matt!"

Dawn rode home with Matt to collect his clothes and toiletries. As he started up the stairs to his bedroom, he called back over his shoulder, "Fix yourself a cold drink while I pack."

"Thanks. What would you like?"

"A cream soda if I have any."

Dawn shrugged. "Whatever you say, boss."

"I wish!" he quipped before disappearing again.

Dawn found glasses and ice and poured them each a soft drink. Too keyed up to sit, she wandered through the downstairs rooms, taking this opportunity for a better look. Somehow, when Matt occupied a room, she didn't notice too much else.

The soft earthen tones soothed, the masculine proportions comforted. She felt safe in these rooms. The telephone rang and she hardly jumped at all. Upstairs, Matt's voice, calm and confident, drifted back to her.

He came back down shortly, carrying his bags. "Lisa called. She didn't spot anyone following us."

"She didn't *what?*"

"Buck gave her a quick lesson in tailing," he explained, "and told her to cover us when we left in case your admirer followed. Evidently he didn't."

"This is crazy. I don't want Lisa involved."

"She already is," he reminded her, ever the pragmatist. "You live with her, he has her number, and he probably knows she works at the bank, too."

She set her drink down and turned away, clutching her arms tightly across her body to ward off the sudden chill. "I hate this!"

"Me, too, sweetheart." Matt pulled her into his arms and held her. "We're going to get this guy, don't worry."

A wave of nostalgia swept Dawn as she made room in her closet for Matt's things. It had been a long time since a man's clothes had hung next to hers. Not that Dave ever wore suits. A sport coat and clean blue jeans had been his idea of formal dress.

"Isn't this cozy?" Matt teased as he stepped out of the small bathroom.

Wasn't it just! "Don't get any ideas, Ivans."

"Too late, I already have the ideas, lots of them."

"Out." Dawn pointed to the door.

He looked comically crestfallen. "Out?"

"Out."

He dropped his head and shuffled out the bedroom door like a large chastised puppy. She closed it firmly behind him and twisted the lock, but when she dropped to her bed to kick off her heels, she couldn't stifle an amused chuckle.

Her smile duplicated itself on Matt's face when she emerged from her room several minutes later in shorts and T-shirt.

"Wow! And here I thought you looked great this morning."

"You've had a rotten day. Go take it easy, Dawn," Lisa ordered, adding with a grin, "Ivans, leave her alone and set the table."

"Yes ma'am." Matt shot to his feet to do Lisa's bidding. After dinner he shooed both women from the kitchen and did the cleaning up.

"He's domestic, too," Lisa whispered under cover of the television's noise. "You really ought to think about keeping him."

A scowl furrowed Dawn's brow. She'd been thinking along the same lines and didn't like it. "I thought you detested him," she reminded her sister.

Lisa shrugged. "That was before I got to know him."

"Know him?"

"Well, I know him better than I did. Mostly what I know is that he wants to look out for you and that makes him fine in my book. Besides, he's got one fine-looking bod."

Dawn snorted and her sister giggled.

"Anybody want more iced tea?" called a masculine voice from the kitchen.

One good look at the small sofa told Matt his large frame wouldn't rest comfortably there, so he made a pallet on the floor with his sleeping bag and pillow. Lisa insisted he fold a quilt under it to make his bed softer and Dawn brought him sheets.

"Are you sure you don't want to sleep in my room?" Dawn visualized Matt's bedroom with its king-sized bed as she looked down at his makeshift accommodation.

He looked up and grinned wickedly.

"Alone," she clarified and playfully threw the folded sheets at his head.

"You're no fun at all," he grumbled.

"Matt, be serious, I can sleep on the couch."

"No, this will be just fine. I want to be out here by the doors and the telephone."

"Okay, see you in the morning." She couldn't help feeling guilty about the whole thing.

"Do you shower at night or in the morning?"

"Why?"

"Suspicious little thing, aren't you?" he teased. "I only want to know when I can use the shower."

"I usually shower in the morning, but you take first choice, it's not a problem for me."

"Me either, so I'll shower now if you don't mind. Go on to bed, I'll try not to disturb you."

Dawn nodded and turned toward her room. She lay in her bed listening to the intimate sounds of him brushing his teeth, the running tap, his soft humming as he readied himself for sleep. She dozed off to the lulling whisper of the shower.

Suddenly wide awake, Dawn didn't know what had disturbed her. A fragment of sound. Feet scuffing over carpet. Someone was in her room! Her bedroom door swung stealthily inward and a large shadow filled the opening.

She stifled a panicked scream, so that it came out as more of a yelp. The shadow turned towards her, and she froze, her heart slamming against her ribs so hard she couldn't breathe.

"Matt," she whimpered, her voice strangled, unable now to utter that life saving scream.

"I'm here, sweetheart."

He was. He really was. "You scared me to death!"

"I'm sorry, I tried to be quiet." He came and sat on the edge of her bed, his hair still wet from the shower, his skin warm and smelling of soap.

She drew a shaky breath and tried to still her trembling. "It's not your fault. Guess I'm still strung a little tight."

"Come here," he ordered as he pulled her up. "Now relax."

It took a minute, but she did as ordered. His flattened palms made soothing circles over the tightened muscles of her back, caressing, gentling. Soon her head slumped forward.

He stroked up her back to her shoulders and neck, kneading the tension from her body. She sighed. His large warm hands massaged the tense cords of her neck, then slid long fingers up from her nape through her hair and over her head. Dawn moaned with the deliciousness of it.

"Feel better?" he whispered.

"Mmm, much, thank you."

"Well, I don't," he complained softly, "so I think I'll go to my lonely bed now. The one on the hard floor."

Dawn chuckled.

He lifted her chin. "But first . . ."

She barely had time to protest, but wouldn't have anyway. She wanted this kiss, needed it, as much as he, maybe even more. His lips were warm and comforting. His touch soothing, not insistent, simply a tender gesture of parting for the night, seeking to assure peaceful rest. A heart-shattering experience for Dawn.

Buck stopped Matt and Dawn as they came in to work. "Anything new?"

Matt glanced at her for verification before answering. She shook her head. "No, not since yesterday."

"He waited a couple of days between the first two calls, it's probably too early," Buck replied.

"It could be that you're making too much out of this," Dawn suggested. "He's probably moved on to more interesting prey."

"You're probably right," Buck agreed.

"We can hope," Matt added.

But the look the two men exchanged told Dawn neither of them believed it.

Chapter Twelve

The telephone shrilled. Matt fought his way through the cobwebs of sleep to stumble to Dawn's bedside. He shook her. "Telephone."

She mumbled in her sleep and pulled the cover over her head. Matt glanced at her clock and shook her again. 1:00 A.M. "Dawn, the phone is ringing."

"The phone?"

"Yes. At this hour, it's probably him."

She dragged herself from the cocoon of slumber and into a sitting position. In the next room, the telephone pierced the night with its shrill summons. She looked up and whispered, "I don't want to answer it."

The light from the living room lamp shone softly on her face and revealed the look Matt had come to hate—the look he'd come to love. That bewildered, beseeching, bewitching appeal that radiated from the chocolate depths of her eyes. He dropped to one knee and laid a hand along her cheek. "Sweetheart, I don't want you to answer it either, but it's the only way we can catch this creep. I'll be right beside you. You can hang up anytime you want."

She rose reluctantly and padded to the phone. "Hello?"

"What took you so long," the man demanded in a raspy whisper. "Did you think I'd give up?"

At the sound of his voice, a heavy weight settled in Dawn's

148

chest. The tape recorder was going and Matt called the telephone company from his cellular phone to start the trace.

"Or maybe you're just so worn out from partying with Ivans that you didn't hear the phone, is that it, Dawn?"

Dawn's palms began to sweat. Her head throbbed, her temples pulsed with the accelerated pounding of her heart.

"Ivans isn't such a big deal," he hissed. "Give me a chance to show you how good I'd treat you."

She couldn't listen passively to another word. Dawn slammed the receiver down before she burst into tears. "I . . . I'm sorry," she wept. "I jus . . . just couldn't take anymore."

Matt put an arm around her shoulders and guided her to the couch where he pulled her down beside him. "It's okay, sweetheart, it's okay. You did fine," he soothed.

"No . . . no, I didn't, I didn't keep him on long enough." Her voice broke and she began weeping harder in spite of a valiant effort to control the sobs. "He . . . he makes me feel so guilty, like . . . like somehow it's m . . . my fault."

Furious with the unseen culprit who'd tainted Dawn's world, Matt dragged her onto his lap. He wrapped her tightly in a protective embrace, tucking her head against his shoulder, holding her close, pretending he had the power to keep the ugliness at bay . . . hoping against hope that he'd have the opportunity to meet this creep face-to-face. If she would only marry him, he could keep her safe where things like this wouldn't touch her!

Her sobs continued, unabated.

"Shhh, sweetheart, it'll be okay. None of it's your fault, you know better than that. Shhh, shhh, now."

He crooned softly in her ear, rocking back and forth with her on his lap. Back and forth, arms locked tightly around her. Back and forth.

Back and forth.

Finally, she quieted, with only an occasional hiccupping breath. She was asleep.

He sat like that with her for a long time, his cheek resting on her bowed head. He'd finally experienced what she was determined to avoid. The reason behind her refusal of him—

the pain of love. Not only could the one you love inflict pain, but her pain became yours as well.

He knew, because at that moment he suffered such soul searing agony on Dawn's behalf, he wanted to howl with it. But at the same time, he knew he'd never want to give her over to anyone else's care.

If love hurt, so be it. He would gladly take on any burden in her behalf, no matter how difficult or how painful. It was his right, she belonged to him.

Dawn moaned and stirred. He'd lost track of how long they'd sat like that, her slumbering on his lap. She tried to wiggle free.

"What's the matter, sweetheart?"

"I hurt," she mumbled.

Matt thought she might be dreaming. "Where, what hurts?"

She struggled against his hold. "My arms hurt, and my ribs."

Chagrined, Matt loosened his hold. "That better?"

"Um-hum."

"Do you want me to tuck you in?"

Dawn opened her eyes and looked around. "What . . . ? Oh, Matt, I'm sorry, why didn't you wake me?" A light flush climbed her cheeks. "Your legs must be dead from lack of circulation."

"Not really," he lied, "but I guess I squeezed you a little too hard. You ready to go back to bed?"

She yawned and stretched her arms. "I guess I'd better."

"You don't have to, if you don't want to."

She hesitated, then softly admitted, "I don't want to be alone."

"Okay, you won't be."

Dawn trusted him to give her just what she needed, nothing more, and he would. He followed her to her room and pulled back the covers for her, then crawled in beside her, dressed in the jogging shorts he'd worn to sleep. He stretched out his arm and she pillowed her head against his shoulder, snaking her own arm across his bare chest. With her curled trustingly against his side, they both fell fast asleep. His last waking thoughts were of the sweet scent of honeysuckle and the brush of silken hair against his skin.

Matt roused to the smell of coffee and frying bacon, his left arm numb. He turned his head and his nose encountered a silky curtain of hair, fragrant on the pillow. Dawn. He'd slept the night with her wrapped protectively against him.

Coffee? Lisa. He groaned. He'd have to go out there and face Dawn's sister, and no way would that little snip believe he hadn't taken advantage of the situation. Gently extricating himself so as not to wake his sleeping bedfellow, he brushed a shadow of a kiss across her forehead and eased out from under the covers.

In the bathroom, he splashed his face with water and combed his hair. Stealthily retrieving jeans and a shirt from Dawn's closet, he returned to the bathroom to dress.

Lisa glanced up when he closed the bedroom door. "Good morning."

He eyed her warily. " 'Morning."

"He called last night?"

"How'd you guess?"

Lisa nodded to Dawn's door and he felt his face heat and his jaw tense. "It's not what you're thinking."

"It's exactly what I'm thinking." Lisa chuckled quietly. "Here." She handed him a cup of coffee.

"All right, so what *is* on your active little mind then?" He sat down at the small round table.

"That character called again, nastier this time, shaking Dawn up pretty bad. She didn't want to be alone with her fears, so you played security blanket."

He nodded, surprised at her accurate diagnosis. "Nothing happened."

Lisa grinned at him. "I know that."

"Oh you do?"

She leaned back against the counter, her arms crossed and continued to grin at him. "Yeah, I do."

"How?"

"If it had, you'd be looking disgustingly smug, not guilty as sin."

Matt threw his head back and laughed, forgetting about waking Dawn.

Lisa threw a potholder at him. "Shhh, you big oaf!"

"What's going on in here?" Dawn stood blinking in the morning light as she fumbled with the ties on her terry-cloth robe.

"Your sister's giving me a lesson in mind-reading."

Dawn observed the two smiling faces a minute, then commented sourly, "If it involves the two of you, there isn't much subject matter to work with."

Lisa looked at Matt and confided, "She got out on the wrong side of the bed. You must have taken up her side."

Matt nodded in sober agreement. "You're probably right. I'll have to remember to sleep on the other side tonight."

Dawn's jaw dropped and her face flamed red. "Now just a minute," she cried, fists planted on her hips.

"It's too late," Matt interrupted. "Lisa knows the whole story."

"There's nothing *to* know!" Dawn protested.

Matt grinned. "Yep, that's what she knows."

"What?"

Lisa and Matt both started laughing at Dawn's outraged confusion. Disgusted, she whirled and stomped back to her room.

"Uh-oh," Matt murmured.

"Yeah, uh-oh," Lisa agreed. "You'd better go get her or we're both in for it for the rest of the weekend."

"Broods for a while, does she?"

"Especially when she's down or not feeling well."

Pushing back his chair Matt winked at Lisa. "Wish me luck."

The bedroom door stood open a couple of inches so he gave it a gentle push. Dawn had her back to the doorway and didn't hear him enter. "Why me?" she whispered. "Why does everything happen to me?"

Matt leaned back on the door, closing it. She jumped as it

snapped shut. "What's your definition of everything?" he asked.

"Everything," she repeated. "The caller, Dave, Julie, you, just everything."

He frowned. "I don't think I like being lumped in the same category with an anonymous caller and a faithless husband. Julie, on the other hand, is a different matter, unless, of course, you're referring solely to her death. If you included the love and joy she brought you, then I wouldn't mind."

Dawn just stared at him dumbly, her expression too weary for words.

"I'm sorry if our teasing was ill-timed, sweetheart. We didn't mean to upset you." He closed the short distance between them and brushed her hair back from her face. "Lisa and I had been joking with each other when you came in and you just got caught in it. Okay?"

"Joking? You and Lisa?"

"She's really not such a bad kid. She loves her big sister and that makes her pretty okay in my opinion."

"Funny," Dawn mused, "she said pretty much the same thing about you not too long ago."

"Oh? She's even brighter than I thought."

She glared at him and turned away. "I'd like to shower now if you don't mind. You'll have to excuse me."

"I don't mind at all, I'll wait right here. In fact, I'll even wash your back if you'd like."

"Matt, please, just go away for a while. I'm not in the mood for your tacky remarks."

He gently took hold of her slumped shoulders. When he dipped his head and dropped a kiss on the side of her neck, he felt her tremble in response. "Sweetheart, calm down, give yourself a break."

His hands slid to the muscles between neck and shoulder and he began to knead the tension from them. "We didn't do anything wrong and Lisa knows it. She knows you so well, she described exactly what happened without giving me a chance to say a word."

He spoke slowly, his voice as much a caress as the hands

that gently massaged the tightness from her muscles. "As for me, I'm just glad I could help; that you *let* me help. Of course you know I don't plan for that to be our one and only time sharing a bed, but I can wait until you're ready. I think."

A giggle erupted, to Dawn's own surprise, at Matt's bleakly uttered "I think."

"That's better. Now get your shower and we'll plan something fun to do today that doesn't involve telephones or morbid gifts."

He gave her a gentle push toward the bathroom, then left the room, closing the door behind him.

"It's all decided," Matt announced when she came out, freshly showered but again in her bathrobe. "Lisa and I voted for Six Flags."

"Six Flags? I don't think I feel up to—"

"Oh, pleeeze, Dawn," Lisa cajoled, "I've already called Doug and everything. He'll be here in twenty minutes."

Dawn shook her head. "Now I know what it means to be steamrollered."

"If you really don't want to go . . ." Matt left the sentence unfinished.

"No." She chuckled. "I won't be the wet blanket. If you kids want to go to Six Flags, we'll go to Six Flags."

"And ride the biggest roller coasters?"

She smiled at Matt. "And ride the biggest roller coasters."

Lisa chimed in. "And the fastest spinning things?"

"And the fastest spinning things," she agreed.

"And eat the biggest cotton candy?" Matt begged.

She broke down laughing. "Enough already! We'll do it all!"

Matt and Lisa cheered, joining arms and swinging each other around the small living room like a couple of ten-year-olds. Dawn continued to laugh at their antics as she went to get dressed. Through the closed door she could hear their friendly chatter as they teased each other, and it struck her how different this Matt was from the one dubbed Ivans the

Terrible; the one whose motives she'd mistrusted when he wanted to take her to Austin.

Stunned, she dropped to the corner of her bed. She couldn't imagine the man she'd gone to work for spending a day at the amusement park just to give her a needed distraction. She couldn't imagine the man who'd yelled at her and issued threats of firing, holding her on his lap for hours when she'd cried herself to sleep. And she certainly couldn't imagine that man lying beside her or any other woman, solely for the purpose of providing comfort and security.

As for clowning like a kid and dancing her younger sister around the living room . . . it didn't bear thinking about. Dawn shook her head in wonder. He loved her. Matt really did love her!

Saturday, Six Flags with Matt, Lisa and Doug, then Sunday, flying in Matt's plane followed by a stop at a roadside tavern where a friendly, oversized proprietor made her feel like a long lost relative. When the three of them piled out of her car at the bank on Monday morning, Dawn felt as refreshed as if she'd returned from a week's vacation.

Matt held the big glass door open for them, then put a protective arm around Dawn's waist as he followed her in. His touch seemed natural to her now, after living in close quarters with him for four days.

The gossip mill went wild when someone saw Matt squeeze her arm as they parted ways at the fax room. He stopped to collect the sheets of paper, while she went on to put away her purse and retrieve his coffee mug.

Her telephone remained silent all day, but Matt received several hang up calls which she suspected came through her old number. He didn't mention them to her, but she was aware of them nevertheless. She knew he reported them to security.

It came as no surprise then, when a package arrived for her late in the afternoon. Buck called Matt first then Dawn.

"Why don't you just let us open it," Buck suggested. "No sense putting yourself through anymore than you have to."

She hesitated. She didn't feel right about letting someone else face her unpleasantness for her.

"It's no big deal," Matt prompted. "Why give the creep the satisfaction of upsetting you?"

"Okay, have at it." She sighed. "But if it's candy, it's mine."

Matt chuckled dutifully at her attempted humor and kissed her forehead. "That's my girl. I'll be back shortly."

Slightly bemused, she watched him go. *"That's my girl."* And he'd kissed her . . . right there in the office! It had felt so wonderful, so right.

Get a grip, Dawn, you don't need a man remember? She remembered, but maybe it wouldn't be so bad just to have one on the fringes? One to have a little fun with occasionally. One to remind her that she was a woman?

Buck shook his head. "Are you sure we're dealing with a grown man here?"

Matt chuckled in spite of himself. "Yes, unless she has two secret admirers? She hung up before we could get a trace on him Friday night," he added.

Buck and Matt stared at the florist's box on the table in front of them. "I guess I'll do the honors," Matt said as he reached for the box.

A frown was on his lips when he folded back the green tissue. Inside three dead roses were tied with black ribbon. Gingerly, he removed the card. It said only: *Nice talking to you.* A tightening sensation clenched his chest.

He tossed the paper across to Buck to read. The older man grunted. "Maybe we'd better hook her phone back up. See what develops."

Matt didn't especially care for that idea, but bowed to the other man's greater experience. "What about that call-back feature the phone company has?"

"What about it?"

"Well, if a caller hangs up, the connection is broken, right? But if the recipient hangs up the line stays open."

"So?"

"This guy evidently hung up right after Dawn did, so we

didn't get our trace. But what if we have that call back feature put on Lisa's phone and on Dawn's line here? We can call back to whatever number placed the call and keep the line open long enough to trace it."

"He's probably using a pay phone, but it's worth a try."

Dawn glanced up at Matt's approach. "No chocolates, huh?"

Matt chuckled, but the sound held no mirth. "Afraid not, just dead roses."

"What'd the note say?"

" 'Nice talking to you.' Can you believe it?"

She patted the corner of her desk and he propped one hip on it. Unconsciously seeking reassurance in the contact, she laid a hand on his knee and pinned him with her gaze. "And?"

He hesitated, then admitted, "Okay. He's upset that he can't reach you through your old number here, so we're going to reconnect it to your line. We'll use the call-back feature to try to trace his calls."

Matt lifted her hand and folded it between his own two large palms. One thick index finger began tracing her delicate bones as he compared her small hand to his own. Her fingers, so long and graceful, the nails femininely shaped and polished, the bones narrow and fragile belied the strength of the woman herself.

"I know you're tired of fooling with this guy," he said, so we're going to bring this thing to as quick a close as possible."

Matt lay awake on his pallet, waiting. 1:45 in the morning. If there was going to be a call it would come soon now. The "gift" and message revealed the man's impatience to talk to Dawn, so he'd probably call tonight.

Rrring.

Even though he'd been expecting it, the shrill sound startled Matt.

Rrring.

Cold fury gripped his stomach as he threw back the sheet.

Rrring.

He opened Dawn's bedroom door, his mind screaming for the obscene noise to stop.

Rrring.

Dawn's feet hit the floor and she met him halfway across the room.

Rrring.

She brushed past him and hurried into the living room to snatch up the receiver.

"Hello." Dawn held the instrument so that he could hear the conversation, too.

"You sure took your time," the now-familiar voice hissed. "Did you get my message?"

To Matt's amazement, Dawn snapped, "You know I'm a sound sleeper. If you want to talk to me in the middle of the night you'll just have to hold your horses until I get to the phone!"

Shocked silence hummed along the line for several heartbeats before it was broken by a surprised chuckle. "So, little Dawn has some fire to her after all. I like a woman with spirit."

"I'd think your tastes would run more to the clinging helpless types," she retorted. "They intimidate easier."

Matt grabbed her arm and squeezed it in warning as he shook his head vigorously. Dawn just wrinkled her nose at him.

"You're pushing your luck," the whispered voice snarled. "You don't want to go making me mad."

"Why not? You've made me plenty angry."

Matt made a muffled sound of distress.

"I've changed my mind. I don't like your spunkiness after all, you've got a smart mouth on you."

"Fine by me. Go find some other way to get your jollies, like pulling wings off flies, you creep."

"It isn't nice to call people names, honey. You think I don't know about you, Dawn, but I do. Your goody-two-shoes act is just that, an act. I know about your shotgun wedding."

He paused at Dawn's quick intake of breath. "So, what's your point?" she managed.

"I can forgive and forget. You and I could have a good life together, but only if you don't make me mad."

"Thanks, but no thanks," Dawn replied flippantly.

An undisguised laugh rolled through the telephone line. "This isn't an invitation, honey," he hissed, "it's a promise. You *will* show me the proper respect. I'll see you soon."

Emotionally exhausted, but triumphant, Dawn smiled as she dropped the receiver into place. She'd done it! Instead of running scared, she'd managed to stay with the creep long enough for him to terminate the conversation. She raised her gaze to Matt, but her smile died under his ferocious scowl.

Gripping her upper arms, he shook her a little for emphasis with every word as he shouted at her, nose to nose. "Don't ever, and I do mean *ever*, pull a stunt like that again, do you hear me?"

He released her and spun away in agitation. "I can't believe you did that. I thought you were a reasonably intelligent woman," he ranted. "If it wouldn't defeat the intent of protecting you, I'd strangle you with my bare hands!"

Lisa's tousled head poked around her door. "What's going on out here?"

"What's going on?" Matt thundered. *"What's going on?* Your big sister has just spent the last several minutes doing her level best to infuriate a raving lunatic!"

Lisa blinked then observed dryly, "And it worked, huh?"

Dawn slapped a hand over her mouth to muffle a giggle.

Matt stared speechlessly at Lisa for a moment then roared, "Not me, you twit, the mutant who keeps calling her on the phone!"

"Oh," Lisa drawled in understanding. "No wonder you're so worked up." She faced her sister. "I thought you, of all people, would have better sense than that. What were you thinking, for Pete's sake?"

Dawn started laughing and the two enraged expressions melted into masks of disbelief and concern.

"Dawn, sweetheart, are you all right?"

"Calm down, sis, I'll get you a sleeping pill or something," Lisa murmured placatingly.

Dawn looked from one worried face to the other; they obviously thought she'd gone round the bend. "I'm fine, really," she assured the pair. "Don't you get it? Can't you see? He didn't scare me. He didn't make me run and hide, I fought back."

She dropped to the couch, leaned back and crossed her arms over her chest. "We're going to get him, I know we are."

The telephone rang and Lisa grabbed it. "Hello? No, everything's fine, just a difference of opinion. I know, I'm sorry. Thanks for checking."

Hanging up, Lisa grinned at Dawn. "Mrs. Hardesty requests we keep our differences of opinions quieter, or limit them to a reasonable hour of the day. She also offered to send her son over to escort the gentleman out the door if we need such assistance."

Matt groaned. "I need a drink."

"There might be some vodka under the sink and there's orange juice in the fridge," Lisa offered.

"I'll skip the vodka, and take the o.j. straight," he growled. "What about you, Dawn?"

"No, I told you I'm fine."

"Well, I'm not!" Matt snapped and headed for the kitchen.

Dawn swallowed another chuckle as he stomped off. She and Lisa joined him in the kitchen and sat down with bowls of ice cream while he downed a quart of orange juice.

Chapter Thirteen

"Matt, he knows I've been married."

"I heard."

Dawn glanced at Lisa. "He also knows about Julie, at least that I'd had a baby."

Lisa's spoon stopped halfway to her mouth. "But how?"

"I don't know."

Lisa thought a moment. "It wouldn't be in your personnel file unless you added it under 'other pertinent information.'"

"I didn't."

"Have you told anyone at work about it? You know how things spread around there."

"No." Dawn paused. "Only Matt."

Both women looked at him and he shook his head. "I haven't betrayed your confidence."

"Are you sure, not even to a close friend? I didn't swear you to secrecy, you know."

He smiled at her attempt to lighten their mood and reached across the table for her hand. "You didn't have to."

"Well, tell Mr. Adams to add it to his list of clues."

Matt nodded. The trio sat in silence for a while, the adrenaline rush fading and the late hour pulling at their eyelids. Lisa had nearly dozed off at the table when Matt spoke.

"What made you do it?"

"Do what?" Dawn asked.

"Go on the attack tonight."

"I don't know. I guess the initial shock of the situation's worn off. It's not much of a surprise anymore; we pretty well know when he's going to call. It made me mad that he threatened me, though. He's trying to imprison me with fear, and I won't have it!"

"But you're not afraid now?" Lisa asked incredulously.

"Nope."

The group that shuffled out to Dawn's car in the morning showed a definite lack of spring in its step.

At the bank, curious eyes followed Matt and Dawn as they made their way to their work station. Rumors abounded and on her floor, Lisa was stopped every few steps by someone wanting to know the latest details.

That night at dinner a nonchalant Lisa asked, "Have either of you heard anything from the kidnappers yet?"

Two heads snapped up and two faces stared blankly in her direction. Simultaneously they asked, "Kidnappers?"

Lisa laughed. "Yeah, kidnappers, you know, the ones who have your son."

Matt looked at Dawn in utter confusion, but Dawn just shook her head. "I think I detect a grapevine story here."

"Give the girl a prize," Lisa cheered.

"Let's hear it," Dawn prompted. "What are the gossips saying?"

"One story has it that you and Matt knew each other before and had a 'love child' who has been kidnapped and held for ransom. This, of course, explains all sorts of things: your immunity to Matt's naturally abrasive personality, security's involvement, etc.

"The two of you have been reunited by the tragedy, accounting for Matt's not letting you out of his sight. His concern for his son, and his undying devotion to you, have him half crazy with worry."

Before Lisa had finished her recitation, Dawn succumbed to a fit of laughter, while Matt sat amazed at the intricate quirks of the human mind.

"At least they got part of it right," he grumbled.

Dawn stopped laughing long enough to ask him, "And which part is that?"

"The part about undying devotion and half crazy with worry."

She wrinkled her nose at him. "Well, the half crazy part, anyway."

He just smiled at her. "It's your turn to clean up the kitchen, so if you ladies will excuse me, I'm going to take my shower."

Matt left the room and Lisa threw her napkin at her sister. "Dawn, when are you going to give that poor man a break?"

"Poor man? Since when are you and Ivans the Terrible on such good terms?"

Lisa shook her head in wonder. "You know, I haven't thought of him by that name for quite a while now."

"You didn't answer my question."

The younger woman shrugged. "I don't know. I think it started when he told me he loved you, but having him stay with us has been the eye-opener. I had no idea he could be so funny or so nice. And it's obvious he's really gone on you."

"Lisa," Dawn warned.

"Oh come on Dawn, you've won. You defeated the dragon, he's yours. All you have to do now is accept the trophy."

"And what, may I ask, is the trophy?"

"Matt."

"I don't want him."

Lisa didn't bother to address the lie. "He's not Dave, sis, he won't wander off when you're not looking. Matt's a grown man who takes his responsibilities seriously." She swept an arm in the direction of Matt's rolled-up bedding. "Just look what he's doing for you."

"Does the phrase 'barefoot and pregnant' mean anything to you?" Dawn argued. "That's his idea of the perfect wife. He doesn't believe in women being able to take care of themselves or working outside the home."

Lisa stood and began to clear the table. "Actually, Dawn, with the right man, barefoot and pregnant would suit me just fine."

Two days had passed since the caller's last contact. They expected a call or delivery today. Dawn tried not to think about it, but grew edgier as the day wore on. Matt pretended he'd totally forgotten about the man, but made a point of staying close, touching her at every opportunity. A hand on the shoulder, a pat on the arm, a kiss on the forehead if they were alone. Just so she knew he was close by.

The delivery arrived, a benign floral offering of one red, long-stemmed rose in a cut-glass bud vase. The attached note read: *I'll see you this weekend.*

"Dawn," Matt began, only half in jest, "we've been living together for nearly a week, now. I'd say it's time I took you home to meet my parents. How about flying to Colorado with me after work Friday?"

"What's the matter, Ivans, afraid I might prefer your competition?" she teased.

"This is *not* a laughing matter."

"I know, but he's not going to run me out of town either. Besides, you don't actually think I'd agree to meet him, do you?"

"I sure hope not, but with your new-found aggression, I'm not sure what to expect anymore."

He looked so genuinely worried she couldn't help placing a kiss on his cheek. "Cheer up, boss, I wouldn't dream of making a move without you."

That didn't make Matt feel a bit better. If any moves were to be made at all, he wanted Dawn to be at least two hundred miles away. The eight hundred miles to Colorado Springs would be even better.

Matt guided Dawn's car through the Friday evening traffic as she twisted around in the seat beside him to talk to Lisa in the back.

"What are you wearing tonight?"

"Jeans and that new sleeveless blouse, I think. How about you?"

"I don't know. I thought about wearing my Mexican skirt, it's cooler."

Matt glanced over. "Wearing it where?"

"We're all supposed to go to Fast Freddie's tonight, remember?"

Matt groaned. "I don't think that's a good idea."

"Matt, we talked about it just yesterday and you agreed."

"I know, but the caller hadn't promised to meet you this weekend when we made those plans."

"How will he know where we are? I haven't told anyone at work what we planned, and Lisa made a point of not telling anyone, either. Just the regular gang knows, and none of the rest of them work with us."

"I still don't like it."

"Oh, come on Matt," Lisa interrupted. "What could be safer than one woman with a gang of good ol' boys looking after her? Texas men are very protective of their women as a rule. I think it's because we used to be so scarce."

Dawn laughed and Matt scowled.

"No, really Matt," Lisa insisted. "Doug told them some of what's been going on and they're pretty upset that anyone would do that to my sister. I'd trust our group of guys with my life."

Doug came for Lisa and the four of them rode together. At the pool hall, Matt had to admit Lisa knew her friends. The minute they entered, a couple of Doug's buddies joined them, effectively forming a loose box around Dawn. When she moved to the tables, those two dropped off and three others closed in surreptitiously, maintaining the ring of protection. On the dance floor, at least four couples from their group kept them separated from the rest of the patrons.

Matt was impressed; these boys would do the Secret Service proud. Then he spotted Buck Adams at a corner table, and guessed the young men had received a little professional coaching. He decided he could relax a little.

A lively two-step played and young Billy Johnson asked Dawn to dance. Matt sat back to enjoy watching the couple move in quick synchronization around the floor. With a total lack of bitterness, he watched them perform the steps he could no longer accomplish.

When Dawn swept by, he smiled and touched two fingers to his brow in salute. She looked so pretty tonight. The tiered Mexican skirt swirled in a rainbow of colors and the turquoise gauze blouse emphasized her golden hair. Around her neck she wore the silver heart he'd bought for her in Austin. Tooled leather sandals showcased slim feet and delicate ankles.

The next slow dance found him on the floor, moving Dawn slowly in a close embrace. "You're looking mighty pretty tonight, Miss Dawn," he drawled teasingly.

"Why, thank you ever so, Mr. Ivans," she teased back. "Ah do believe you're about the handsomest man Ah've danced with so far."

Matt's head tipped back as he laughed, and Dawn smiled at her accomplishment, realizing how very much she enjoyed being the one to elicit that warm rolling sound from him. He wrapped both arms around her waist, so she slid hers around his neck. "Much better," he murmured. She thought so too, but wouldn't admit it.

He nuzzled her neck and whispered, "Lady, you drive me crazy."

His breath feathered her skin and his voice vibrated over her nerve endings. Dawn attempted to put some distance between them, but he only let her pull back enough to allow him to reach her lips. A short kiss, but one filled with sweet tenderness. Matt slowly lifted his head and her eyes followed his mouth, trying to figure out the source of his magic.

"Do you know I'm in love with you?" he whispered.

She nodded, breathless.

He smiled. "Good."

When he gathered her against him again using his jaw to press her head to his chest, she couldn't stop the soft sigh that welled up from a contented heart. She didn't know where their relationship could go, but maybe it was time she gave it some thought.

Matt joined Buck at the bar, each man pretending not to know the other. "Glad to see you," he murmured.

"No problem," Buck answered. "Her friends have been very helpful."

"I've noticed. They think a lot of her and her sister." Matt tilted a long-necked bottle to his lips and sipped before asking, "Seen anyone suspicious?"

"Not yet. I'd ask if you had, but it's obvious you can't see past the woman," Buck taunted.

"Yeah, well, what can I say?" A lopsided grin creased one side of his face.

Buck chuckled. "I don't blame you. Enjoy yourselves, you've both earned a little R and R. If I see anything, I'll alert you."

"Thanks."

Billy Johnson approached. "Matt, Dawn's gone to the ladies' room, someone's with her, so don't worry. She says she'll meet you by the pool tables."

"Okay, Billy, thanks."

Dawn emerged from the rest room, accompanied by two of the other women, and found Sam waiting for her. Jabbing a thumb in the direction of the rear exit he said, "Matt wants you outside, by Doug's car. They've found a kitten or something."

"A kitten?" She turned that way then paused. "Are you coming?"

"Naw, you have a guard out there, I'm going to dance with Bev," he said with a grin as he grabbed Bev's arm.

"I'll be out in a minute," Mary offered, "just let me tell John where we'll be."

Dawn stepped out the back door and looked around the dimly lit parking lot, getting her bearings. She located Doug's car and saw Matt crouched near the back studying something on the ground.

"What do you have there?" she called as she crossed the parking lot.

He didn't answer, but raised his arm, motioning her on over. As she closed the distance, an uneasiness gnawed at her but she couldn't put her finger on it. Something about the way Matt moved? No, not that. The set of his shoulders? The shape of them? Certain it had to do with his body language, she continued to wrack her brain.

No, not the way he moved, it was the way he *didn't* move that rang false! Matt couldn't crouch with both knees bent and his weight on the balls of his feet that way. One knee bent and the other to the ground, that's the closest thing to a crouch Matt's bad leg and ankle allowed. She skidded to a halt in the loose gravel.

In one swift movement the man rose, turned, and grabbed her arm, jerking her roughly to him.

"Let me go!"

"Not on your life, honey. You're mine now," the familiar voice whispered. Then he laughed, the natural undisguised sound she remembered from the other night.

"Jerry!"

"That's right, good ol' Jerry. You should have taken me seriously, Dawn. It isn't nice to toy with a man's affections."

As he talked, he dragged her across the parking lot to where his truck waited in deep shadows.

Struggling against his hold, Dawn's mind searched feverishly for something to say that would make a difference. Something that would buy her some time, something that would bring the man to his senses! Only nervous chatter came out. "I take you seriously, honest I do, but you deserve someone without a history, Jerry. You know about me, you know I messed up. What would a man like you want with a loser like me? You deserve better."

She dug in her heels and twisted against his grip to no avail. Her sandaled feet slid in the gravel, and the sharp-edged rocks inflicted stinging cuts to her unprotected flesh.

His fingers bit into her arm with viselike pressure. "Jerry, please," she begged, "you're hurting me." She had no chance on earth of breaking free of his powerful grasp.

"Then stop fighting," he growled, as he jerked open the door and lifted her bodily into the cab of the truck.

Dawn scrambled to the passenger side and grabbed for the

door handle. Locked! Jerry slammed his door. Scrambling frantically in the dark, she located the hole where the locking button should be, but it had been removed. The truck roared to life.

Her fingers skimmed over the door panel searching for the window switch, only to discover it, too, was locked. She turned on him then with an enraged screech, hitting and clawing at him in an unrestrained bid for freedom. She was just getting her life back together. This man had no right to ruin it for her.

Jerry grabbed her wrist with one hand but she managed to turn off the ignition and pull out the keys. As Jerry searched the floor his keys, she kept her feet moving across the floor in an effort to frustrate his search.

Cruel fingers closed around her ankle and Jerry cursed her with a steady flow of invectives but she continued yelling and kicking. Someone had to hear her, had to help her.

Jerry gave a satisfied grunt and her heart sank as she recognized the jangling sound of a key ring. Unwilling to surrender to the inevitable, she reached for the ignition at the same time he did, interfering with his attempts to reach the keyhole.

"Enough!" he roared.

The ominous metallic click stilled her. Even in the dim light, she could make out the shape of the pistol Jerry aimed straight at her.

"That's better," he panted.

Their labored breathing, harsh and raspy, sounded loud in the small enclosed space. With certain dread Dawn saw her life slipping away.

"That's better," Jerry puffed.

He turned the key but nothing happened. In the scuffle, they'd shifted the truck into gear. He cursed, adjusted the gearshift, and tried it again, but just as the engine roared to life, the driver's door flew open and he was pulled sideways out of the cab. The truck leaped forward, the gun discharging with a thundering report as he fell, and Dawn screamed.

Jerry toppled out onto the ground and the driverless vehicle rolled on without him. Faintly, Dawn heard her name called as she struggled to pull herself behind the wheel and gain control of the runaway truck. Another gunshot, another scream . . . not her own this time, she thought hazily.

She managed to pull herself upright behind the steering wheel just as the truck plowed into a light pole, effectively ending its wanderings. She'd struck her forehead on the steering wheel and her head throbbed, but her only thought at the moment was escape. In her haste, she stumbled out the open door and fell, only to be grabbed up by strong hands. She thrashed, oblivious at first to the voices around her.

"Dawn, stop, it's all right, you're safe now," insisted a young male voice.

"Please, Dawn, we need to see how badly you're hurt. Oh Doug, there's so much blood."

The gun's report in the confined space of the truck had left her ears ringing, but she thought she recognized her sister's voice. "Lisa?"

"Yes, yes. Please don't fight us, Dawn, sit down," the girl pleaded.

"I can hardly hear you."

Lisa was sobbing.

Shadowy figures closed in around them, but just before she was completely surrounded Dawn caught sight of a struggle across the parking lot, and of a man stretched out on the ground.

"Matt!" she screamed, reviving her attempts to break free of the helping hands.

"No Dawn, stay here," Doug commanded. "The ambulance is on its way."

She screamed Matt's name again and with a strength renewed by fear, broke their hold, running, stumbling across the dirt and shale to his side. She fell to her knees on the sharp rocks, only dimly aware that four men held Jerry pinned to the ground a short distance away.

Bev knelt on Matt's far side, a blood-soaked towel pressed firmly against his shoulder.

"Oh, Matt, no," Dawn sobbed. "Please be all right. Please, God, let him be all right."

His outstretched arm lifted weakly to embrace her. "I'll be fine, sweetheart," he whispered. "Don't cry."

"It's all my fault. I told you to stay away from me, now look at you."

"Don't say that," he answered, his voice firming. Needing to assure himself of her safety and well-being, Matt strained to see her in the dim light. What he could distinguish did little to ease his mind. Her face and blouse were streaked with blood and dirt, her hair a tangled mess. "You look worse than I do. Let them help you, sweetheart."

Dawn shook her head vigorously in denial, then cried out in pain.

"Okay, okay. Here, lay your head on me then," he coaxed softly.

She curled against him and gingerly rested her head on his uninjured shoulder, oblivious to the fact they reclined on a bed of rocks in a dirt parking lot, surrounded now by over a hundred people.

Dawn's friends kept the curious crowd back enough to allow them breathing room. When shock threatened and Dawn began shivering, someone brought a blanket and covered her and Matt. In the distance, sirens wailed, the sound building as the emergency vehicles drew closer.

Registering their approach, Dawn's anxiety grew with the siren's volume. Once before she'd prayed to the accompaniment of sirens that God would be merciful. Now she did it again. *Please, don't let him die, it's my fault, take me instead. All of it's my fault, Julie, Matt, Jerry, all of it. Take me, God, just please let Matt be all right.*

Chapter Fourteen

The crowd parted, allowing medical technicians and police to swarm over the figures on the ground. In no time, the police had Jerry handcuffed and in the back of a cruiser. Two medics tended to Matt and a third, a woman, eased Dawn away to conduct an examination of her injuries.

Matt cried out a little when they moved his arm, and Dawn tried to get back to him. "Matt! Don't hurt him!"

"Miss, please hold still, he's in good hands. Does your head hurt?"

Dawn looked at the efficient young woman as if she were crazy. "Yes, it hurts!"

"Then don't you think you should sit still?" She fastened a blood-pressure cuff around Dawn's arm. "We'll stay right here out of the way while we take care of you, and let the others do the same for your friend, all right?"

"I can barely hear."

The medic flashed a light past Dawn's eyes, checking the reaction of her pupils. "When did you first notice that?"

"Um . . ." Dawn tried to concentrate. Stunned and confused as she was, the splitting headache didn't help things. "Right after the gun went off, I think."

The technician looked in her ears then gingerly felt her skull for any more signs of trauma. "You must have been awfully close to it."

172

"Yes, in the truck." Dawn began shaking again. "Jerry pointed it at me in the truck. It went off when he fell out."

The woman looked sharply at Dawn. "Lie down, we've got another ambulance coming, then we'll get you and your friend to the hospital."

The medical technician covered Dawn snugly then used her own body to block Dawn's view of Matt.

Lisa approached. "I'm her sister, may I sit with her now?"

"That would be great. Keep her as quiet as you can and I'll see if the guys need a hand with the other one."

Dawn could see one of the men holding a glucose bag in the air over Matt's body, but she couldn't see Matt's face. Her view was blocked by the medic checking his blood pressure and pulse. She hadn't heard any more sound out of him. *Please, God, please.*

The second ambulance arrived in a flurry of dust and noise. The crew jumped out and immediately removed a gurney. Dawn's attendant hastily conferred with the new arrivals then turned back to Matt as the new team lowered their stretcher beside Dawn.

"Hi there, gorgeous." The medic smiled at her, and took a new pulse and blood-pressure reading. She thought drowsily that he had friendly eyes and a pleasant smile. "Well," he said, "looks like you're ticking along just fine, but we'll let the experts make sure, okay?"

He motioned to his partner and the two men gently lifted her onto the stretcher, then raised it and started to the ambulance with Lisa walking along side.

"No! No!" Dawn suddenly realized they were taking her away and grabbed for Lisa's arm. "Lisa, don't let them take me, I can't leave Matt."

Lisa took her hand. "It's all right; Matt's being taken care of. You'll see him at the hospital." She looked to the men for confirmation. "They're going to the same hospital, aren't they?"

"Yes, ma'am."

It didn't matter, Dawn wouldn't be consoled. "Matt! I want to see him!" She sobbed.

"They're about to load him up too, darlin'," the medic soothed, "so don't you worry. Just had to make sure he didn't hurt his arm any more on the trip, is all."

"Don't let them take me," she begged. "I can't go yet. Please, don't take me. I can't see him, please."

She sobbed all the way to the hospital, plaintively murmuring Matt's name in gasping little breaths. "Matt, I want to see Matt." If she kept saying his name, he'd be safe. Nothing could touch him if she refused to let him go. And she would. She would fight to her last breath for him.

Tears streaming down her own cheeks, Lisa rode in the front seat looking back through the window at her sister's ravaged face.

As they were unloaded at the hospital, Dawn and Matt saw each other briefly, then were wheeled into a large treatment room where a nurse drew the curtain between them. Dawn hadn't stopped crying since they'd pulled her from his side, and Matt could hear her muffled sobs even now.

Lisa appeared and Matt heard her trying to soothe her sister as nurses worked to clean up the blood and determine the extent of her injuries. A team of doctors hovered over him, and he knew that soon he'd be taken to surgery.

He tried to talk to them, to ask about Dawn's condition, but they ignored anything he said not directly related to his own injuries. Finally, in frustration, he summoned his strength and bellowed, "Lisa!"

Immediately she poked her head around the curtain. "Yes, Mr. Ivans?"

A half smile lifted one side of his mouth. "Is she okay?"

"She will be. Mostly bumps and scrapes, I think, but she's worried sick about you."

"Pull back the curtain."

Lisa glanced at the medical team and hesitated.

"Pull it back!"

A doctor nodded. The hospital staff melted away to allow the couple to see each other, unobstructed, and Matt winced when he got a clear view of Dawn's battered face. A big lump high over her right eye oozed blood from split skin, and one cheek appeared red and puffy. He cursed softly.

Reaching out he tried to touch her, but his hand fell short by a good ten feet. A nurse glanced at the doctors, then moved quickly to Dawn's gurney and shoved it closer. Dawn's hand shot out and gripped his in a fierce hold.

"I'm so sorry," she whispered brokenly, tears streaming down her face. "I hope someday you can forgive me."

Matt squeezed her hand, cursing under his breath because he couldn't pull her into his arms. "Sweetheart, there's nothing to forgive. Now stop crying and I'll see you in a little while, okay?"

She didn't answer, just clung harder to his hand. Lisa came and whispered in her ear and Dawn nodded. Ignoring the impatient medical team hovering around them, Lisa pushed Dawn's gurney flush against his then helped her sister to sit up.

"Her head," a young doctor protested.

Lisa shot him a ferocious scowl and snapped, "It's what's inside it that I'm worried about." No one else interfered as she murmured to her sister, "Now kiss Matt, then let the doctors do their job. Besides, you'll want to get cleaned up before he sees you again—you're a mess."

Dawn leaned over and Matt pressed her gently to his chest with his one good arm. Suddenly her palms were bracketing his face and she was kissing him with wild desperation, oblivious to her own injuries. Matt tensed his arm, holding her to him, pressing her as tightly as he could in an effort to allay her fears.

"Dawn," Lisa prompted quietly, "we have to go now. The doctors need to sew Matt up. He'll be right back."

Reluctantly she drew away, her beleaguered eyes searching his for the truth of Lisa's promise. "I'll be back before you know it," he assured her.

The operating orderly glanced at the other occupant as he jockeyed the gurney into place. "Isn't this a bit irregular?"

"I'll take full responsibility," the head nurse assured him, winking at her youngest brother and his girlfriend.

Lisa smiled her thanks to Doug's sister and took the chair by Dawn's bedside. Dawn had been given only the mildest of painkillers to ease her physical discomforts and calm her emotional state. She had a slight concussion, a sprained wrist, and an ugly assortment of scrapes and bruises. Other than that, the doctor said she'd be fine. Lisa hoped so.

She and Doug took turns sitting with Dawn through the night in case she woke in a panic, but she barely roused when the nurses made scheduled checks of her vital signs. Physically and emotionally exhausted, she slept until the breakfast trays were delivered.

Dawn opened her eyes, blinked at the light, then frowned at the pain.

"Hello," Lisa greeted, keeping her voice low.

"Ohhh."

"Not feeling too good, huh?"

"My head . . . Who was yelling for a nurse? Or did I dream that?"

"No," Lisa whispered, nodding to the curtain around her bed. "Your roommate seems to be a real grump."

"Just what I need."

"Nurse," the voice thundered, "where are my pants? I will not use this blasted bedpan!"

Lisa stifled a giggle when Dawn's eyebrows shot up. From the other side of the curtained partition they heard the nurse rush in, rubber soles squeaking on the tiled floors.

"Mr. Ivans, please," she hissed. "Your racket isn't helping your roommate's headache a bit, I'm sure. Now please try to be more cooperative or we'll have to move you."

"I've got a hole in my shoulder and you want me to sympathize with a headache," Matt grouched.

"She does have a concussion, you know," the nurse scolded.

"Oh, a concussion, sorry . . . Wait a minute, did you say she?"

Lisa rocked back and forth on the chair, holding her sides,

her lips sealed shut on her laughter. Dawn shot her a furious scowl, the best she could manage in her battered condition.

"Dawn?" Matt called. "Dawn!"

"Please, Matt, not so loud," she groaned.

"Open that curtain," he ordered the nurse, "No, wait! Give me my pants first!"

Lisa gave up the fight and dissolved in fits of laughter. Tears streamed down her cheeks and her sides ached she laughed so hard. Matt continued to fuss and splutter on his side of the room, only mildly reassured by her mirth.

Doug came in and Lisa dismissed the nurse telling Doug, "Help the man with his pants before he busts a gut, then you and I can go home and get some rest."

On Lisa's orders, Doug directed Matt to the bathroom before they'd let him see Dawn. Lisa hurriedly touched up the worst of her sister's bruises with a little makeup and ran a brush through her hair. Then she kissed Dawn's cheek and pulled back the curtain. "See you two later," she promised.

Dawn watched Matt approach her bed, taking a quick inventory as her eyes swept him from head to toe. He had a couple of scrapes and some small bruises on his face, and he needed a shave, but otherwise he looked wonderful. But when her gaze fell to the thick cushion of bandages on his shoulder and the sling that immobilized his left arm, guilt left her tongue tied.

Matt had to swallow a couple of times before he could speak. The gash he remembered from last night had been bandaged, but the lump under it had swelled even more and turned a ghastly purple. A vicious bruise covered the crest of one delicate cheekbone and spread partway around her eye. Her sprained wrist sported an elastic wrap and her arms bore ugly marks from Jerry's iron grip. A killing fury quickly rose to choke him, then he looked into her eyes.

Ah yes, Dawn's eyes. If he'd thought they mirrored her vulnerability before, that word didn't begin to describe what they now held. He'd never in his life seen such utter hopelessness, such complete devastation, reflected in so beautiful a pair of eyes. He couldn't hold her gaze, it hurt too much knowing he'd failed her.

Dawn choked back a sob. "I'm . . . I'm sorry, I'm so very sorry."

His gaze flew to her face and he reached instinctively for her hand, bringing it to his lips. "What do you have to be sorry for? I'm the one who let you down."

"You did not!" A tear slid down her cheek over the scraped and bruised bone. The saltwater stung and she winced. "I nearly got you killed last night."

"Sweetheart, no." He gripped her hand tighter. "You can't blame yourself for a madman's actions."

"But he shot you."

"He might have shot you too." He inhaled a ragged breath and his whole frame shuddered. "I've never been so gut-deep scared in my entire life."

"I'm sorry," she apologized again, but he barely heard her.

"You were taking too long. I went looking for you and couldn't find you." His voice broke. "I'm never letting you out my sight again, I don't care what you say. My heart can't take it."

"I should have just stayed in and never started going out with Lisa." Tears tracked down her cheeks. "I didn't mean to hurt Jerry's feelings, I'm not a tease, honest."

"Dawn, shhh."

But she continued, "And I didn't mean to get you hurt. You've got to believe me, I'd never do something like that."

"Shhh, I know, sweetheart, I know. It had nothing to do with you. Jerry's sick, he needs help. It could have been almost anyone—Lisa, Bev, Mary. It just happened to be you he fixed on." He paused and ran a finger tenderly down her undamaged cheek. "Not that I blame him. I'm pretty fixated on you myself."

Her eyes reflected her shattered spirit, her need for absolution. "No, you were right. If I'd stayed home where I belonged, this never would have happened."

He sat on the edge of her bed and tenderly brushed the hair back from her face with gentle strokes. "No, Dawn, I was wrong. It doesn't matter if you stay home or if you work constructing skyscrapers. No one is absolutely safe from hurt in this life. You did it my way once, you stayed home to raise your child and look what happened. I couldn't have protected you then anymore than I did last night.

"Heck, I can't even take care of myself," he growled disgustedly. "I'm astounded by the utter arrogance I had in thinking I could take care of anyone else."

"But you did, Matt. If it weren't for you, I might be dead by now." She closed her eyes as a small tremor shook her body.

He sat on the edge of the bed and slid his hand under her back, urging her to him. She reached for his neck and wrapped her arms securely around him, careful for his wounded shoulder. "I thought I'd lost you," she whimpered.

"Never," he answered, his voice gruff with emotion.

"Oh, Matt, I was so scared."

"Me too, sweetheart, me too." He brushed his lips across her forehead. "Are you really okay?"

"Mm-hmm. Just the damage you see and a little concussion."

"No need to postpone the wedding, then?"

"No."

He drew back and she smiled timidly at him.

"I love you, Mr. Ivans."

He sat in stunned silence for just a moment, then threw his head back and laughed in great rolling waves of relief and joy. The nurse poked her head in, frowned, and firmly shut the door, setting him off again.

Dawn leaned back on her pillow and enjoyed the sight of him, the sound of him, the warmth of his nearness. Reveling in her love, she lifted a silent prayer of thanksgiving for this second chance.

With an orderly's help, Matt pushed his and Dawn's beds together in the middle of their room. Propped on their pillows, they ate lunch from the trays across their laps and watched the noon news on television. A brief report on the fracas at

Fast Freddie's mentioned only Jerry's name, and Dawn sighed in relief.

A light tap sounded on their door and Matt called, "Come in."

For a moment nothing happened, then the door swung slowly open and a middle-aged man cautiously peered inside.

"Daddy," Dawn squealed.

The man frowned at Matt as he stepped smartly into the room, followed by a woman Dawn greeted with, "Mom!"

"Since when are hospital rooms co-ed?" Dawn's father demanded.

Her mother rushed to her side and planted a gentle kiss on Dawn's cheek, then brushed a strand of hair back from her face. "Look at my baby." She gasped. "Oh my poor darling, are you really going to be all right?"

"I'm fine, Momma, it looks worse than it is. Just bumps and scratches."

"And a concussion," her mother added firmly.

"Only a small one."

"Young lady, I'm talking to you," her father interrupted. "What is this man doing in your hospital room?"

"Him? Oh, he's recovering from a gunshot wound. A barroom brawl, as I understand it. We met in the emergency room."

Matt had eased to the side of his bed, where he now stood. "Dawn," he warned, his voice low.

She grinned at him and complained, "You're no fun. Daddy, Mother, I'd like you to meet my rescuer and fiancé, Matt Ivans."

"He's the one Lisa's written me about, your boss?" Dawn's mother asked with a smile.

"I didn't know she'd mentioned him, but yes, Matt's my boss. For a little longer anyway."

Matt looked at her questioningly.

"I've told you it's bad for your character development to get your way all the time, Matthew," she explained primly. "So sometimes I get to be the boss once we're married."

Her father laughed. "If she's anything like her mother, she'll be the boss more often than not, Ivans."

Matt grinned as he shook his future father-in-law's hand. "That's fine by me, sir. I think I can handle it."

The men laughed together as Dawn blushed a rosy pink, and made a face at Matt.

The doctors released both Matt and Dawn on Sunday afternoon. Everyone sat in Lisa's living room, a cozy group in the small apartment.

"So tell me, what went wrong?"

"Well, Mr. Blyel," Matt addressed the older man, "your daughters' friends were doing a great job of shielding Dawn from all outsiders, but it turned out that the man we wanted to protect her from belonged to their group. He sent me in one direction with a fake message through one of the men, and sent Dawn in the other by the same means. Everyone thought she was still being guarded, until I became concerned that she didn't meet me when expected.

"It took a few minutes to discover what had happened. By the time we rushed to the parking lot, Jerry had her in his truck and was driving away."

Mrs. Blyel gasped. "I still can't believe you girls didn't let us know what was going on," she chided. Dawn sat snuggled between her parents on the sofa.

"Dawn fought so hard," Matt continued, "Jerry had to keep his attention on her, making it easy to come up and pull him out of the truck."

He and Dawn exchanged a conspiratorial glance. No one had mentioned to the Blyels that a gun had been pointed at their older daughter at the time, nor that it fired when Matt pulled on Jerry's arm. No sense in adding to their upset.

"Simple, huh?" Mr. Blyel grunted. "Then how did you get shot?"

Matt shrugged. "Jerry pulled a gun and I tried to get it. It went off in the struggle. The other men jumped him then, disarming and subduing the suspect," he finished in imitation of a police report.

Everyone chuckled, but Dawn. She forced a smile but the memory of Matt sprawled on the ground, his blood soaking into the dirt beneath him, was entirely too vivid for her to laugh about just yet, or probably ever.

Mr. Blyel eyed Matt speculatively for a minute, patted Dawn's arm, then asked, "And she's agreed to marry you, huh? When's the wedding?"

Matt grinned at Dawn, knowing he had an ally in her father. "How does tomorrow sound?"

"Fine by me," the older man agreed, "but I doubt you can get a license by then. How about next Saturday?"

"Great," Matt exclaimed at the same time that Dawn yelped, "Daddy!"

"Okay, okay, how about in two weeks then?" Her father sighed.

Everyone laughed, including Dawn, who found her wedding date set for her.

Mr. and Mrs. Blyel were headed back to Houston, Doug and Lisa talked quietly at the dining table and Dawn napped where she sat beside Matt on the sofa. She roused and lifted sleepy eyes to him.

"I'm so sorry," she murmured.

"You do not have anything, and I mean *anything,* to apologize for," he growled, then lifted a hand to her head, pressing her against his chest. He rubbed his chin in her hair and asked tenderly, "What on earth am I going to do with you?"

"Kiss me," she replied. "I need you to make me whole, Matt. I need to feel normal again, not like the player in some bizarre game." More quietly she added, "Not like a failure as a woman."

His arm slid to her shoulders and hugged her against him. "Not that, sweetheart, never that. The failure was Dave's, not yours. You were a good wife . . . and a good mother."

"I'm not a mother anymore."

"Yes you are," he corrected firmly. "You'll always be Julie's mother. And when you're ready, we'll talk about making you a mother a few more times, too."

She looked up at him, into his warm gray eyes, and wondered how anyone could ever think of this man as terrible. "Really?" she whispered. "You really want children?"

"No more than half a dozen," he cautioned.

She squealed in delight. "Oh, Matt, I love you."

"I know, that's what this is all about, isn't it?"

The late-afternoon light softened the scrapes and bruises that marred her skin, but Matt didn't see the blemishes. He saw only perfection. Inside and out. The heart of a lion, the beauty of Venus, and, he thought, a wry smile twisting his lips, the stubbornness of a mule. But the true kicker, the most incredible thing of all, was that this complex package of womanhood was his. She loved *him,* of all people, and she was his. He threw his head back and laughed, overcome with joy at his good fortune.

"Oh, God, woman, I love you so."

Dawn snuggled close. "Then what's with the giggles?" she asked, her tone petulant.

His hand cupped the side of her face and his thumb nudged her chin up so he could look into her eyes. "Because you make me so happy, sweetheart."

"You're sure?"

"I'm sure. I'll prove it to you, okay?"

"Oh, yes please."

"But we'll have to take it easy," he cautioned.

"Whatever, just hold me Matt, love me."

"Always." He feathered light kisses over her face, but she wanted more. She captured his lips for a deep kiss that left them both breathless.

"Easy," he cautioned, laying his thumb gently against her bruised cheek. "Are you okay?"

Dawn smiled and snuggled against him. "More than okay." She sighed. "We both are."

And she knew it was true. Theirs would be a partnership of love; neither dominating, neither controlling, they would share that special world known only to the very blessed.